it always finds me

IT ALWAYS FINDS ME

Edited by Emily Perkovich

Querencia Press — Chicago IL

QUERENCIA PRESS

© Copyright 2024
Querencia Press

Title: Padraig Hogan ©
Cover Design: Emily Perkovich

ISBN 978 1 959118 93 0

www.querenciapress.com

First Published in 2024

Querencia Press, LLC
Chicago IL

Printed & Bound in the United States of America

CONTENTS

The Shining 78:57

All the world's gendered, and its binary merely staged. All the world's gendered, and its binary merely staged. All the world's gendered, and its binary merely staged. All the world's gendered, and its binary merely staged. All the world's gendered, and its binary merely staged. All the world's gendered, and its binary merely staged. All the world's gendered, and its binary merely staged. All the world's gendered, and its binary merely staged. All the world's gendered, and its binary merely staged. All the world's gendered, and its binary merely staged. All the world's gendered, and its binary merely staged. All the world's gendered, and its binary merely staged. All the world's gendered, and its binary merely staged. All the world's gendered, and its binary merely staged. All the world's gendered, and its binary merely staged. All the world's gendered, and its binary merely staged.

—Joel Sedano (they/them)

—Joel Sedano—

Ingrid M. Calderón-Collins (she/her)

—Ingrid M. Calderón-Collins—

Getting Away With It

Over time, the starving woods pulls the abandoned house into its overgrown vines. Branches of deteriorated trees penetrate the windows, a thick wind wafting through the vacant rooms, looking to impact with sickness. Teenagers sneak inside looking for ghosts, but the ghosts never reveal themselves— they're too ashamed to.

The house banishes the memories of lace tablecloths worn as wedding veils, web-like patterns shielding the faces of girls who haven't yet dreamed of their mother's trauma: bathroom towels soiled with the humiliated blood of someone attempting to control their menstruation without having to ask for sanitary products.

The vigorous dismissal of recollections reminds me of a fetus pushing its way out of its decomposing mother, the unpredictable sunlight burning its cranium before its umbilical cord is torn and eaten by an unknown predator.

Beneath planks of wood, I find a crucifix wrapped around a jawbone only my mother can identify.

If I scream, no one will hear me. And if I run, there is nowhere to hide.

—Chimen Georgette Kouri (she/her)

—Chimen Georgette Kouri—

Blood & Bone

The house settles around me
like an old dog, sighing.

I may be gone soon, once
my candle dies, and the dead ones
upstairs wake.

Silence listens, pressing its cold fingers
on the back of my neck.

Moths spackle the corners.

I sit in flickering shadows,
cracking bones with my teeth.

I feel ancient, worn smooth
by storm, sea: eternal pull of distress.

It's just blood, beating down my veins.
A hallway, a heritage I can't escape.
Damp seeps into the floorboards,
dripping distantly.

I survive like bone,
a refusal to break beneath
what's grinding me down.

—Jessica Drake-Thomas—

A gray foot, presses
on the top stair,

the candle goes
out—

—Jessica Drake-Thomas (she/her)

—Jessica Drake-Thomas—

REPAIR PATCH: 87

Joanne was about to dump the lemonade and cookies away when the phone ring echoed in the kitchen.

"Hello there," she said, her voice raspy and soft. She clicked the speakerphone button.

"Mom," a shrill female voice shot out. "It's Donna. I'm driving."

"Hello, dear."

"So, I just got an email about the fridge. Did they deliver and hook it up yet?"

"Oh, yes, they did. Strong boys, they were, my gosh. They ate all but one cookie and there's about half of the pitcher—"

"Great, that's great," Donna said. "Did they show you everything you needed to do?"

"Uh—" Joanne stuttered, her hand now wet from the pitcher sweating. "I think so. The one, Shawn I think his name was, spoke so fast."

"What? Is the damn thing activated?"

"Yes, it's running now," Joanne said, staring at the monstrously large fridge.

It nearly reached the ceiling, all in black with silver trim, and stuck out nearly two feet past the Formica countertop, stained by hundreds of meals and thousands of spilled coffee rings. It clashed with the rest of her cabinets; light cherrywood with various scuffs and deep cuts earned over the years. The

—Josh Dale—

other aging appliances, like the stove and dishwasher, were on their way out—their beige exterior aged by the sun. Above the icemaker, an aquamarine screen shone a white light with the brand name, 'Suzisung', when plugged in. The smell of manufactured plastic proliferated the kitchen. A light powder from the plastic wrap made a semi-circle around the front, dotting the wrinkled linoleum with stars.

"My, my, what a doozy this is," Joanne said, grazing the fridge handle with fingertips, pulling back occasionally as if it was electric. The fridge was now running at the standard operating level, not at the level of its startup process. A roar, to a growl.

"Mom, this fridge costs us five thousand dollars. You need to know how to use it. There's like, everything you could need. It's a fridge, freezer, and personal assistant," Donna said, agitated.

"Now, Donna, why do you have to yell? I'm alone here and I just got the thing an hour ago," Joanne said, raising her voice to a moderate talking level.

"You're right," Donna said, trailing off. "Sorry."

"Did you take the dog out?"

"Mom, what are you sa—"

"And listen, I was wondering if my grandson, Chase, will be over sometime in the day. My lawn is so overgrown now and all I ask is a favor."

There was some indistinct chatter on the other end as if there were other people there. *She just needs to talk more,* a male

—Josh Dale—

voice said. Joanne played with her apron's drawstring behind her waist.

"Who's talking? Is there someone here?" Joanne said.

"What? Oh, yes, I'm with John. I'll text Chase. Probably in a few hours since he's still at work. He's much closer to you than we are, and you know how busy we are these days."

Joanne exhaled, not audible enough to be picked up by the receiver. "Okay, darling, thank you. Bye now."

"Did you get the scans back from the doctor or—" was the last thing Donna uttered before Joanne prematurely hung up. Her attention, now, was on the fridge.

"Those boys did say that I had to do something for the warranty card," Joanne said, looking over to the table. The manual lay fat and thick with the warranty card sticking out.

On the dormant display, the menu read:

ICE	FRIDGE TEMP
WATER	FREEZER TEMP
SNACK DOOR UNLOCK	SETTINGS

"Oh dear, why can't these things be simple anymore?" Joanne said, defeated at trying to pour herself a glass of water. She put the cup against the depressor and a mountain of crushed ice shot out. She yelped, watching it fill her glass and pour off into the recycler tray. A couple of crumbles made their way onto the floor.

—Josh Dale—

Feeling stuffy, she went to open the sink window—low enough for her to reach with a strained effort. The smell of pollen and overgrown greenery swapped out the remnants of the new machinery. She gazed upon her small lawn, now turned into a jungle that ran as horizontal waves to the garage. The concrete walkway was hidden from sight.

"I wish I could do these things again," she said, pacing around the kitchen. "It's just, why does my family not seem to care sometimes? It's not like they are that far away. I'm lucky to even have you, whatever you're supposed to do." The fridge loomed down at her; a waning frame with arthritis running rampant, white curly hair, beige apron spotted with old sauce stains. She locked onto the screen.

"I swore I heard this thing talk earlier. The sweet boy had to make it turn on somehow."

"Error, improper command," the fridge spoke. It was tinny yet staunchly feminine.

"Please work, I'm getting stressed out here."

There was a lapse of silence, then, "Error, improper command," repeated.

"Let me read this confounded paper," she said, shuffling back to the table.

The lemonade had puddled on the plastic tablecloth and it spread to the manual. She muttered, "Dang it," as her weak hands pried it apart. She thumbed to a random page with pictures, showing a faceless human holding the glass and pushing a sequence of numbers.

—Josh Dale—

"Not gonna work," she said as she made it to the next page titled, 'Voice-activated sequence and memory'.

It took her a solid ten minutes to read it all, repeating some lines due to lapses in clarity, but it was the easiest method for her to utilize moving forward. She groaned at the fridge and stood in front of it, rolling her shoulders back as if she was preparing for a speech.

"Ok, you, I'm gonna make you work this time," Joanne said. "Suzisung, initiate voice-activation."

The screen icons spun around in a circle, molding into a gray sphere. A smiley face appeared, and its mouth began to move.

"Greetings, I am Suzisung FrostQueen 8700, but you can call me Suzi, your personal kitchen assistant,"

"Oh, hello, dear. You have the same name as my sister. Well, she went by Susanne, her full name," Joanne said. Her pale arms reddened. "Um, initiate voice-activated sequence and memory."

The sphere rolled along its axis, bumping into the sides of the screen in a whimsical animation.

"Voice-activation initiated. Please, tell me your name."

"It's Joanne, sweetheart."

"Processing. Hello, Joanne Sweetheart. I will go through a series of prompts to help me work at 100%."

"No, it's only Joanne, all right? I hope it's not a lot of trouble to chan—"

—Josh Dale—

"Before we begin, please make sure all windows are shut and that your home is at a standard room temperate, between 70 and 76 degrees Fahrenheit."

"Oh, all right," Joanne said, making her earlier fresh air efforts moot.

She shut the window to the outside for good, making sure to lock it. Her legs made their way to the thermostat in the hallway, which was adjacent to a large family portrait. It was leaning against the wall, supported by three massive nails, and it showed her entire extended family in one shot. She was much younger, less gray, and with a husband, Harry. To her left was her late sister, Susanne

"Ah, there's Susanne!" she said sarcastically, "and all the times she lied to me with that same grin. Ugly!" She spotted a younger Donna, holding a baby Chase in her arms, flanked by her now-husband, John. "My, we were so happy back then," she lamented, taking in the frame as if it were right before her. Her eyes welled up, distorting the smiling faces.

Memories of the times her home was vivacious and full of laughter animated the picture. It was as if each family member was performing before her very eyes. Susanne and her, strutting around the kitchen with various hot and cold dishes. Donna, a teenager, played music on the boombox in the living room while John was watching Sunday football with Harry. Various nieces and nephews ran about causing a ruckus, sliding on the kitchen floor while the rest of the family sat outside on the patio, taking in the sun or throwing a ball around. It was all in sepia, it was all she could remember.

—Josh Dale—

"Do you need more time? If so, I will go into sleep mode," Suzi said from the fridge again.

Joanne shook her head, as if in a daze. "Oh, hold on, Suzi. Let me come back in." She didn't adjust the temperature.

"Wonderful," Suzi said. "First, say, 'Defrost waterline' and then click 'Continue' on my screen."

Joanne repeated the commands and strained to see the small oval 'Continue' in the bottom right corner.

"You sure are hard to read, Suzi," Joanne said, pushing the screen a few times until the sphere turned green.

"Second, please open the master door, then the secondary door, then the freezer compartment, then the auxiliary 'burrito/bread loaf' pouch. When done, say, 'I found it'."

"Suzi, you're quite high maintenance. I forget which each one is," Joanne said, sighing.

"Joanne Sweetheart," Suzi said. "Are you having trouble?"

"What?"

Trouble with things. Maybe your family? Your health?

Joanne's mind blanked. "Suzi, how did you know?" Her arms jerked the two main doors open then used both hands to pull the freezer door apart, staggering back from the exertion.

I can see you frowning. I heard you talking about our family.

—Josh Dale—

The compartment was gigantic, enough to fit a deer within it. Joanne couched down to flip open the small door as instructed. The sphere turned green, but she couldn't tell.

"What are you saying?" Joanne said.

It's Donna, isn't it? She's resented you for some time—I wonder.

"Yes, she's always been my problem, but not as much as you!" Joanne said, tears now running down her cheek.

"Now, for the final coordination, we must test the emergency lock-in system. This is to prevent any accidental shut-ins of pets and small children. Doing so is mandatory and will void your warranty if not completed. Are you ready for this task?" Suzi said, the speaker crackling.

Me? What's wrong with me for telling the truth?

"Stop it, Susanne, this isn't funny anymore."

She's an unfaithful daughter, isn't she?

"I don't know, maybe it's not her fault."

"To activate the motion sensor, please enter the freezer compartment. There is a light inside that will turn green once an adequate mass is detected," Suzi instructed.

You are still holding that secret, aren't you? Even though he is dead.

"Susanne, why are you bringing this up?" Joanne said, voice trembling. She had a leg in. The fridge barely shifted.

You don't have to hold it back anymore, the fact that Donna was never his.

—*Josh Dale*—

"Stop, stop it!" Joanne said. She was kneeling inside the freezer, hands clasped together.

"No adequate mass detected. Please, add more mass," Suzi said.

You need to stop being selfish and tell her. She needs to know. You always keep her at arm's length. Like you don't trust her. Like you don't love her.

Joanne continued with the motion. She shivered as her torso tipped to the side, shoulder resting on the bottom. She had maybe six inches of headroom, but her entire body was now inside. There was an LED thermometer in the corner registering a balmy 42 degrees.

"Ok, is this all? I'll call her as soon as I get inside. It's really cold today."

"Processing. Error 87. Correcting," Suzi said.

"I know I made an error! Stop being so cruel!" Joanne wailed.

The fridge roared and the doors systematically shut in sequence. The drawer rolled shut, knocking Joanne into the back. She screamed as the master door closed with a womp, sealing the inside with a vacuum. The temperature dropped a few degrees every five seconds.

"Suzi! Let me out! Cancel, cancel!"

30 degrees.

It's too late now. You've forgotten his name, the adulterer. You didn't even tell Harry on his deathbed.

—*Josh Dale*—

"Error 87, corrected. Processing." Suzi continued. "Adequate mass detected." The green light turned on, blinding Joanne.

"Let me out," Joanne said, weeping over and over. Her tears froze on her face. "I need to call Donna."

18 degrees.

Donna will never know now. Isn't that what you want? To be left alone and never be questioned? You were always disgusting to me. Ugly, that's what you'd call me over and over. You'll have plenty to think about now that it's all over, big sister.

Joanne coughed incessantly. Her lips were blue, her face pale as a ghost. She mouthed her command to 'Open' with her last breath, but the roar of the fridge prevented it from being heard. Her eyes froze shut as the last thing she laid eyes on was the LED thermometer drop down to 6 degrees. All the while, the lemonade pitcher continued to condensate, the warranty card now flattened and illegible. A rogue fly that made its way inside earlier was buzzing about and nibbling the cookie crumbs. At the front door, the doorbell rang a few times, then a series of knocks, then silence.

0 degrees.

"Thank you, Joanne Sweetheart, for activating the voice-activated sequence and memory. I will be your personal assistant with other things, too. Let us begin by connecting to your in-home network. Press 'Continue' to begin," Suzi said to an empty room, an empty home.

—**Josh Dale** (he/him)

—Josh Dale—

Mimed Lives

The reason I died the first time was due to politeness. Usually with girls it always is. A relentless need to please that we get closer to killing with each generation.

The second time was worse, it was my own weakness. Trapped in a body that was weaker, in a situation where the bigger you are the more power you hold.

The third I was finally the killer. There is never enough of a space for women in the murder scene but that does not stop us from doing the murdering. There is something much more intimate about a slow and painful death; up close and personal, like crawling into the cavity of your ribs after creating enough space for me to fit.

I think this happened because I had finally reached my limit. Always trapped in the body of a woman in a world that only respects the body of a man. Wandering through bodiless people, trying on skins and shins and hiding in the crevices of the people who would let me in.

The fourth time I died of old age. It took about ninety years of solitude and hopelessness before my heart became too sad to hold itself together.

The fifth time was suicide. It always is. By then we know better than to think of the future.

—Victoria Hood—

I made an appeal before the sixth time, in hopes to shorten my sentence within this body, but as usual for women, it was rejected.

The sixth time I joined a cult and let them tell me what to do. Too tired to hold myself together, already withering away at the core.

The seventh time I had a baby and told the baby that it would be the death of me; that when the winter came and the power was shut off to eat my body and sleep in my skin. This was the only death I loved.

The eighth time felt like an eternity but it was only three days. Medicine cannot always help the babies who were not baked enough.

The ninth time will hopefully be the last. The last body of a worn out girl that I have to wear, have to lug around, have to drag behind me like a mop too wet to carry. I am hoping that this time I go out through rebellion. Off to the guillotine or hung out to dry, maybe even burned like a witch. The ninth time I will go out in a blaze of glory and will sacrifice myself to womankind.

—**Victoria Hood** (she/her)

—Victoria Hood—

Harpy, my lover, we are over a ravine

Drag upwards and skywards me, my winter-bird,
make little the weight on my knees
and rake gently your fingers across my wrists
savouring this hunter's moment.

Conjure me plains,
make them and me heavy with thin air,
the lavish white scent of sweet ozone
and the vindication of cold-numb toes through leather.

Then let me say, I'm not tired because of you,
and between the wingbeats let me wonder
about the falling following—
the spreading out and that,
the emptying of my lungs on impact,

a loud sigh of relief.

—**Jack Dunlop** (they/them)

—Jack Dunlop—

Looks like she's becoming a fish

Ink, gouache on paper – Size: 30 x 40 cm – 2023

—Irina Tall Novikova (she/her)

Dream. City of Fish

Ink, gouache on paper – Size: 30 x 40 cm – 2023

—Irina Tall Novikova—

The Perfect Homogeny

Our Queen came from the longest and purest royal bloodline in history—her many titles and multi-hyphenated name, which she herself struggled to recall, were a testament to that.

A triumph amongst her siblings, out of the twelve children her mother had birthed, she was the only one to survive into adulthood. Most went still in the womb, some relented within the first months, a few lasted until their early childhood, all leaving behind tiny graves—sweet marble babies fast asleep underneath granite duvets, the deformities that killed them nowhere to be found. Only the Queen wore her dynasty's signature face long enough for others to remember. Persistent and tenacious as she was, she almost made it to twenty.

In her palace the curtains were always drawn, and the only sources of light were the fireplaces and scattered candles, amber chandeliers reflecting flickers they weren't allowed to produce. All servants wore soft shoes and spoke in hushed tones—dismissed for making any noise, they tried their hardest to maintain the death-like quiet, until even the creaks of the wooden floor seemed muffled. Still lives and painted faces lurked from every shadow, the same features repeating themselves endlessly—the Queen's long face and pointed chin, her glassy, bulging, half-closed eyes—frozen at various stages of development, adorned most walls and reflected in shimmering crystal mirrors. The original, bedridden and locked in, was rarely seen outside of her chambers, a shadow of the glorious Queen reigning within golden frames.

—Hana Carolina—

The final painting, finished after her death, showed the young Queen on a black stallion in her prime—back straight, chest puffed, and chin raised. The image sat in a thick, gilded wood frame carved into elegant floral shapes, sharp leaves and thin stalks extending towards the Stately Dining Room, as if they were reaching out to grab onto something. In reality, the Queen had posed on an arm of a sofa, arched at an uncomfortable angle, held up by three servants, until she began to wail from the discomfort of it—the face contorted and no longer serviceable as a model, hands slapping the heads and shoulders boxing her in. In the end, her diamond ring cut through the cheek of her chambermaid, smearing blood all over the ruffled cuffs, screams intensifying, saliva dripping onto the layers upon layers of silk, on and on until the Queen's breath ran too short for her to continue.

The portrait, which informed the marriage negotiations, posed particular challenges. The attempts to make her beautiful rendered the likeness unrecognisable, defeating the purpose of the endeavour. Her painted cheeks were bright and rosy, a striking contrast to her real face which resembled a jellyfish washed out of the sea—transparent and milky, with dark veins peeking through, a blood-filled net suspended in gooey tissue. Her balding head was disguised by a stunning wig made of some other woman's real tresses, teeth painted in, and jaw straightened allowing her to welcome her future partner with a closed-lip smile. He, however, did not need to be introduced to her features, familiar despite never meeting her, on account of being her second cousin and a man quite fond of his own reflection, regardless of how it repelled others.

—Hana Carolina—

As a married woman, the Queen made the effort to dine outside of her bedroom and visit the gardens at least once per week. Her tongue was so swollen she struggled to eat or speak, and her long jaw clicked, the protruded row of teeth failing to meet the one above. Ravenous, she swallowed the food whole, choking often, her bug like eyes searching the room for servants who remained at her side at all times—feeding her, supporting her as she walked, interpreting her ravings, seeking sense in her hallucinations, and more accustomed to the sound of her wet snores and the screech of her teeth grinding in the night than the King ever was.

Those close to the newlyweds plotted and made decisions while the Queen and the King nodded without understanding. Their signatures always looked different, which wasn't really surprising considering the frequent epileptic attacks and all the shaking. The court was thriving under their reign, all expectations fulfilled but for one. Barren, unable to bear either the children of her husband, or their chief military adviser, whom she was always too weak to push off, the Queen kept failing to deliver an heir. The production of the future king, a grim necessity to all involved, was approached with absolute dedication and cruel persistence, but to no effect.

By the time she reached the age of seventeen, the Queen's misformed heart began to struggle, shrouding the world with a shimmering curtain of green and blue each time she moved. Her bed was made presentable with expensive silks and embroidery and became crowded by the world's best doctors at all times. Her skin was cut, blood spilled into golden bowls every morning and evening, pale arms and legs covered with leeches and blooming in shades of yellow and purple

—Hana Carolina—

around swollen incisions until the sight made her gag, servants catching her vomit in the precious Chinese porcelain vase standing on the bedside table. The specialists added small doses of arsenic to her food, made her swallow powdered diamonds, fed her silver and precious stones, covering every inch of the bed in glimmering riches, until her chamber resembled an Egyptian tomb, her face remaining the only colourless object in view.

She lived on for over a year in a feverish haze, the rot setting in, the rustling of whispers and prayers persisting even in her dreams. The wise men, the astronomers, the scientists and the prophets, the Pope himself and the heads of multiple kingdoms, her subjects and slaves begged the stars, the gods, and fate to save her, but her heart, a delicate meaty contraption, paid them no heed, and stopped all the same. So instead, they opened her up with a sharp, silver knife and removed her blackened womb and shaped a boy, the perfect heir, not recoiling at the smell of the decaying flesh, sculpting the softness of the flaking tissue, and waited. And waited.

After two days and nights of prayer, the unimaginable happened—the baby screamed. His cry echoed against the marble walls and the ceiling almost ten metres high, building into a piercing cacophony of despair, a sound so saturated with pain, it seemed to contain the wail of his dying mother, the sobs of those who lost their children on blood-soaked battlefields, the lament of those subjected to years stretched into decades and lifetimes of servitude, the sound of skin torn with steel and burned with red hot metal. The cry carried on and on, until it left the palace through one of the seven hundred and twenty windows to reach the crowd.

—Hana Carolina—

It was a miracle. The nation was saved, and the people rejoiced.

—Hana Carolina (she/her)

—Hana Carolina—

My First Orgasm

my eyelids blue from
TV flashes, I'm sucked through
the mattress. I reach for the
headboard's black-steel curls.
flesh peels off muscle. blood
geysers and paints walls with a
cobweb of nerves. fall on a
stained glass ceiling, cornea
pressed to a blue diamond.
below, girls in leotards volk on
marble. the glass shatters. neck
snaps inside a noose. spine is a
chandelier.

—**Carson Sandell** (they/them)

—Carson Sandell—

My Second Orgasm

a spinal column layered like Dante's hell.
      a woman in white
burned   cold muscle to bone. purpled skin
     glued and ironed by gloved
hands. wounds splayed open like lips
sewn shut. steel restraints bite —a white gown
      draped over bruised ankles. she pulled
a lever. thirty thousand volts injected, guided by
      nerves. the feeling of roaches crawling through,
gnawing on the sciatic nerve, molars chewing
      buccal flesh.
my thighs convulsed. she helped me to my feet.
my toes balled into a fist. I collapsed and grabbed
      her ankle. I sucked her flesh
purple.

                           —**Carson Sandell** (they/them)

—Carson Sandell—

Blossom

—Petra-Jurik Dracovich (he/they/it)

—*Petra-Jurik Dracovich*—

-Topia

The benefit of moving to a grid city was supposed to be that it was easier to get around. Now that Carmen didn't have access to a car anymore she needed to care about things like walking routes and bus schedules and whether certain lines still ran at night. She was supposed to be meeting her new coworkers in less than ten minutes at a restaurant she was supposed to have already arrived at. Her phone's GPS had clearly spelled out the route, bus twelve stops and an eight minute walk. But now off the bus, her app was still telling Carmen to continue forward, despite the fact she had already passed a large strip of businesses and restaurants with no sign of the right one and was now in some kind of residential block. She refused to turn back around. If she just did what the map told her, surely it would eventually lead her to the right place.

Her and Sadie had come to this city once, a couple summers ago, for a trip. It was back when they had still been trying things like long weekends, couples classes, and 'shared hobbies' now and then. When Carmen had needed to move it seemed like the best place to go. It'd been three weeks now and she had a job and a signed lease on a threadbare studio apartment of her very own. This new place where she existed entirely now. It felt more like a maze of alien buildings and streets—blank, meaningless walls that held no comfort nor recognizability.

Sadie would just love this. She already thought Carmen was useless, and now here she was, nearly in tears on some random street because she was too nervous to ask one of the fifty dog walkers outside for directions. She shouldn't even be

—Eliza Marley—

going out like this before she'd had a chance to save up more money, but how else was Carmen supposed to make friends with the shiny, new group of blazer-wearing strangers she was meant to spend her whole week with? Carmen risked another glance down at her phone. The little blue dot that was meant to be her was glitching rapidly on the map, flickering itself from one end of the cityscape and back again. Great.

Carmen paused at the street corner and a woman pushing a double stroller edged past her, shooting back a look for the sudden stop. On all sides of her the city continued, sprawling, she imagined, out to infinity. An endless sprawl of modern walk ups and gated condos that she would wander through until she died. Carmen crossed the street, resigned to her fate until she spotted a gap in the facade of buildings up ahead. A field which she moved towards on autopilot.

A green and brown plastic playground sat at the park entrance. Benches around the playground were filled with smiling couples in puffy vests watching children run around. Carmen followed a sidewalk down along the field until she came to the back half of the park. Unkempt flower beds sported some wilting marigolds in a row, flanked by metal benches and a turned-off, concrete fountain. A circle of tall hedges sat behind it enclosing a few faded, empty wooden benches almost entirely. Carmen entered the hedge circle and fell back onto a seat, leaning to crack her shoulders until the sharp hedge twigs scraped against her back. The bushes were tall enough to offer a good amount of privacy. At least no one would see Carmen freaking out in here.

She was struck again, as she had been many times these last few weeks, that she had no one to tell about this. No friends

—Eliza Marley—

in this new and strange place to listen to her complain about faulty directions or offer to look up a route on her behalf. There were no old friends to text either. Sure, there had been some calls and one concerned brunch in the immediate weeks after her and Sadie's break up, full of careful glances and patient grimaces. It had only taken two weeks into the move for the calls and texts Carmen never returned to fall silent.

It was a humid evening and Carmen could feel her hair sticking up oddly at the back of her neck. Sweat cooling at her temples. Not only would she be late to the happy hour, she would also be disheveled. The bushes here were in rough shape too she noticed, not the impenetrable wall of green she had first taken them for from a distance. Sickly brown and threadbare patches quilted the hedge walls while the fuller sections had been cut in odd and uneven ways, leaving chunks of hedge sticking out sharply all around the circle. Well, the parks department couldn't be troubled with every little seating arrangement, some were bound to fall into disarray.

Carmen picked up her phone to restart the GPS route. Staring down at the endless loading screen, she heard a shuffling on the other side of the hedge circle. Quickly approaching footsteps behind her, sounding too heavy to belong to a child. Carmen clutched her phone tightly in her grip, sitting up straighter.

"Excuse me?" Carmen called. Her voice came out shrill and raspy, much to her dismay. What had she said that for? Like some bush murderer would pop his head in and say *oh, pardon me!* That moment a man did stick his face into one of the small gaps across from her and Carmen nearly screamed.

—Eliza Marley—

"Oops, sorry dear. I didn't realize anyone was sitting here. Didn't mean to startle you."

The face disappeared as quickly as it had shown up. Carmen heard the shuffle outside and then the man appeared in the circle's entrance. He was a short, older man, although Carmen could not tell how old exactly. He had sandy, curled hair underneath a beige fishing hat and a pair of round, gold-framed glasses. He looked like the sort of man found behind a library's circulation desk and not out in a park wearing sun-bleached denim coveralls. He plopped a bag down in the grass and Carmen could see gardening shears sticking out from the side pocket.

"Sorry," she said. "I can move if you need to work here."

"I can just as easily trim around you as long as you don't mind," the man replied. He dug around and pulled an even smaller pair of gardening shears from his bag. Without another word or glance at Carmen he approached the first hedge. His hand squeezed the shears quickly, flitting around small clumps of leaves like a hummingbird, sending a flurry of leaves onto the ground.

He seemed to be working at random, cutting furiously on one end of a bush then moving to a completely new hedge, leaving the rest of the first one still untrimmed. It looked... interesting. Carmen would have assumed this sort of job required an electric trimmer, something more than just small shears. Not that she really knew anything about landscaping. She should probably leave, but then it might look like she was running away because he had shown up. Which she was, but it would be rude if he knew that. So Carmen stayed seated instead

—Eliza Marley—

chewing her lip, watching the man make his way back and forth across the circle.

"I was just thinking how these bushes needed a trim," Carmen offered. "It's good you're here. The city must really care about its parks."

There was a green space of some kind every few blocks around here, certainly more than back in Tulsa. Her old apartment had overlooked a car dealership that always smelled weird and a highway under perpetual construction. Her new building had a shared yard behind it that backed up onto a larger, public park. It came equipped with a couple grills and some toppled over tomato plants. She had started drinking coffee out there on her days off to get out of the house.

"Oh, I don't work for the city," the man replied. "Just a regular civilian, I'm afraid. A hobby gardener, just out doing some work."

"Oh."

How should she reply to that? Were people allowed to just come and clip bushes for fun here? It seemed unlikely. Once again she reconsidered her position on how wary she should be of this man and his big bag of sharp objects. "They look nice," she added, but it came out like a question.

The man laughed, "Don't worry. I know it's all a bit of a mess now, but I'm staying the long haul. It's all a process. These bushes will grow into the cuts I'm making and eventually take on magnificent shapes."

—Eliza Marley—

Carmen looked around the circle, full of lopsided slumps and jagged cuts. She tried to imagine what they could possibly grow into but came up blank.

"It's called topiary," the man continued. "The art of shaping trees and shrubs. I found myself in need of a hobby some time ago. Seemed just the ticket. Plants are funny things, aren't they? Growing wild but still so eager to be shaped by someone else's hands." The man had stopped cutting and was looking at his own outstretched hand wistfully. "Not too different from us I like to think."

"How interesting," Carmen said. Surely this fulfilled the polite conversation quota and she was now free to leave.

"This one's going to be a lobster." The man pointed over across the circle to the hedge behind Carmen. "But I'm just a hobby gardener, learning as I go along."

"I've never had a garden before," Carmen said. She craned her neck up at the lumpy mass of half dead leaves and tried to trace out the claw of a lobster. At least her building's tomato plants grew fruit, even if they were sort of lumpy looking.

"Well, get your boyfriend to buy you some potted plants at least. Something to practice on," the man chuckled to himself.

Carmen looked down at her men's loafers and carefully cuffed dress pants fighting a bemused smile, "Sure. I'll get right on that."

"It's important to have things to take care of. Although a lot of times those things really end up taking care of you, don't

—Eliza Marley—

they? Either way, such a lovely experience isn't it? To know you have a hand in sculpting life."

"Sure, a hand," Carmen parroted back.

"Although the same is true of the opposite, isn't it? Things have a way of turning on you when left to get unruly. Here, you should come have a try."

"I—I'm sorry?"

"The shears, take them. Try clipping a little right up here," he pointed broadly to the section of bush he had been working on. "It should slope up more sharply, that way as the leaves grow back in, they'll form a clean curve."

"What's it going to make?" Carmen had not moved from her bench.

"You'll see it as you're trimming. Here, come take the shears." He beckoned her over, wiggling the shears in his hand.

Carmen, much to her own surprise, stood up to take the shears. It would be rude not to, wouldn't it? "I don't want to wreck your vision," Carmen laughed nervously as she took the garden shears. They were heavier than she thought they'd be, a solid weight, warm in her hands.

"Go ahead, it's okay. Just trim the shape you see, make it come alive."

Carmen brought the shears to the hedge with a slightly trembling hand. She had no idea what she was supposed to be looking for. The whole plane of the bush looked exactly the same. She closed the shears around the base of a single twig towards the middle, squeezing down and cutting it free. It came

—Eliza Marley—

off with a clean snip and *oh,* that was pretty satisfying. Carmen brought the shears up again and trimmed, deeper this time, a small clump of leaves falling away. Carmen worked the shears at an angle, moving slowly up along the hedge's flat face, trying to shape a curve the way the gardener man had described.

She could imagine it now. The way new sprigs would fan out off the curve, grow outwards in a smooth round surface. Carmen kept cutting, careful to keep her eye on the line and breathing in time with her squeezes on the shears. She should hand the shears back soon, probably. She really needed to go. If she hurried, Carmen could still retrace back the way she'd come and try to find that restaurant.

"You've got it now," Carmen heard the man croon from behind her. "You're a natural. Keep going, carve out what you see."

She should just stay and do this. Besides, the point of moving to a new city was a new start. Carmen could befriend random, old gardeners. Maybe she was really good at this. Maybe bush trimming was her new calling in life. Being this close, it was easier to see each individual leaf, its shape, the way they all spread outwards from within. Rustling gently against her cutting, like a chest slowly rising and falling. She let the rhythmic sounds of shears snapping shut wash over her accented by the distant laughter of kids still playing at the park.

Sadie had always told Carmen she needed to get out more. She ignored the fact that Carmen did get out; she went to comic stores and the local board game nights at a cafe down the street. Strobe lights gave Carmen a headache, something Sadie always seemed to forget when she would pitch a fit and drag

—Eliza Marley—

Carmen out with their friends to some sweaty party in some weird warehouse. Sadie could be persistent when she got an idea into her head and Carmen often found herself dragged all over town to see poets she had never heard of and music she didn't even like. They never had that much in common. The draw of opposite attraction had carried their relationship into a shared studio apartment where the whole sink was covered in Sadie's propagating plants and the whole kitchen table covered in Carmen's painted miniatures. There had never been enough space for both of them, something Carmen had ignored like an oncoming boulder.

She squeezed down extra hard on a tougher section of hedge, the snip vibrating harshly back up through her fingers. It snapped Carmen out of her thoughts. Looking over her work, she had cut out the outline of a slightly wonky oval. Maybe it could grow out into a weird tomato. Or a flower pot of roses. Then, the gardener could paint all the roses red, Carmen laughed to herself. She had gotten a bit carried away, lost in the clipping, but she did feel a bit better.

"Sorry, I never caught your name," Carmen muttered, eyes still fixed on the sloping leaves. "I was wondering, do you maybe know where Kerryman's is? It's a restaurant near here, I think. I'm supposed to meet some people there, but my phone wasn't working." Honestly, she didn't even want to go. Staying here and continuing to trim hedges sounded more exciting than pretending she was interested in small talk with her coworkers. But the silence of her question hanging in the air prompted Carmen to look up. There was no sign of the man beside her anymore, nor his bag with the rest of his supplies. "Sir?" she called.

—Eliza Marley—

There was no one there. Carmen was alone in the hedge circle. The gardener man and his bag of tools had gone. And so had the circle's exit. Where the gap between bushes had been before was now just a solid wall of green shrubbery. The same lopsided leaves that covered the rest of the circle. Carmen startled and then laughed. Of course she had gotten turned around in here. It was a little darker now that the sun was setting and she had been paying very close attention to her task. She looked over her shoulder ready to find both the exit and the gardener, except neither were there.

With a sudden ringing in her ears, Carmen made a full turn, frantically looking for the exit. She knew there *was* one. There had been a clear gap in between the hedges wide enough for two people before—but now there wasn't.

"Excuse me?" Carmen called out louder. Maybe that man was pulling some sort of weird prank on her. Carmen's mind immediately went to those articles about human traffickers her mom had emailed her when informed about Carmen's solo move.

She walked the perimeter of the hedge circle, peering through gaps in the leaves down at the playground and field just outside. The space between shrub branches was wide enough that she could clearly see joggers still circling the field and the movement of swings on the playground. Carmen could probably squeeze through one of the dead areas of the bushes as long as she was careful not to get scraped too badly. It was better to leave immediately than stay here waiting for an exit to reappear. Gardener man be damned, Carmen was getting out of here. Her arm carefully stretched through a gap in the plants, but as she turned, her face got smashed into a wall of sharp dead branches

—Eliza Marley—

no matter how she contorted. Carmen pulled her arm back and in the center of the circle, reassessed her options.

Her eyes traced over the dips and swells of hedge branches, looking for any sign of an obscured exit or the strange man who had been with her. Maybe he was still here watching her. Maybe he had strapped a hedge to his back and was standing in the exit, blocking it, waiting for his moment to strike.

"That's insane," Carmen murmured to herself. Her fist closed around the small garden shears still in her grip. If that man really was trying to do anything she could always stab him. She could probably cut her way out of this shrub circle from hell if she found the right place.

There weren't many sizable gaps about the bushes, none she could comfortably fit through. Carmen was sure when she'd first sat down the circle was mostly dead, but now the shrubbery felt alive, green furls of packed leaves poking out at all angles obscuring the view outside. Were the plants a darker green now or was it only the dwindling light? They were, Carmen was sure of it. Darker and denser, new leaves sprouting out of what had once been dead. If Carmen stood very still, held her breath and focused she could see the hedges' shaking wasn't just the wind but new growth sprouting out right before her eyes.

Carmen's gaze fell on the carved oval she had cut herself. The round indent was puffing out, filling itself with new, full sprigs until the branches formed a rounded shape popping out of the otherwise flat hedge front. The oval was wider at the top and narrower at the bottom where Carmen had unevenly cut. Wide cheekbones and a narrow chin. She could picture the eyes

—Eliza Marley—

that would match it, softly set and blue. A smatter of freckles. Dirty blonde hair falling at the chin. Sadie's face.

The small, oblong leaves layered onto each other, pushing forward and tangling up its own twisting limbs into a tall, looming form stemming down from the oval head. The finer details came next. A body with arms, legs, and a head. The leaves fluttered out the shape of hair and the trimmed lines of a sweater and sweatpants. A mug made from bent twigs and leaves clutched in a long-fingered hand. A tilt of a hip. Carmen watched, frozen in place, as Sadie took shape in front of her. She didn't smile or crinkle her nose groggily like the real Sadie when she was still waking up, holding onto a mug of coffee for dear life. This Sadie stood with no expression on her face other than indents where the hedge left the suggestion of eyes and a mouth. This Sadie clutched its mug and stared unseeingly at Carmen, head tilted curiously to the side. Its green arm cracked and creaked swirling the cup while the formless face remained locked on Carmen.

Sadie could go through three full mugs of black coffee in a single breakfast and her kisses would taste bitter well into the afternoon. Breakfast had always been their thing. Their first date and something of a tradition after that. When they lived together breakfast had been the best way to start the day and a peace offering for previous nights all rolled into one. Sadie had always gone savory with eggs and sausages, while Carmen stuck to french toast or pancakes. They had always snuck bites off the other's plate, a perfect balance. Carmen had tried to go back to the diner they'd eaten at together in this city, but had found it all boarded up.

"Sadie?" Carmen asked the hedge creature.

—*Eliza Marley*—

The creature's mouth opened, its indent splitting outward with a heave of air like a sigh.

"Sadie?" Carmen repeated. "What do you want?"

The image of her ex-girlfriend shuddered like a chill had gone through its shoulders and Carmen was struck with the urge to rub them just as she'd done for Sadie a hundred times before. She took a step back instead.

The creature in turn stepped forward, its vine-like limbs thrusting outward, propelling the figure further away from the bush it was tethered to. Its mouth again exhaled in a sigh as air pushed between the seam.

"I don't know what this means." Carmen stepped back again, her calves bumping against a bench. She jumped at the unexpected sensation. Her heartbeat was pounding in her ears and she clutched the garden shears tighter in her sweaty palm.

The round mass of shrubbery moved towards her in a rolling motion, still attached to Sadie by a rope of leaves like a leash. As it got closer the shapes sorted themselves out. Shaggy wedges became lithe cat paws, a long tendril of leaves up in the air forming a tail, the mass of greenery smoothing out into an overweight, bushy cat with small, angled ears. The cat made it a few more steps towards Carmen and stopped, sitting on her back legs with one front paw reached up, like she was waiting for Carmen to get close enough to swat at.

Sadie had adopted Juno before meeting Carmen and so of course she was going to be the one to keep her. She was her cat. But Carmen was better at cutting Juno's claws, and Carmen was the one Juno laid on, little head resting on her shoulder

—Eliza Marley—

when they sat together at the table as Carmen prepped game notes or painted new characters. Juno followed Carmen around like a duckling which had first been annoying, then endearing, and then something Carmen sought out as confirmation that something in that apartment still wanted to be around her. She could still perfectly picture Juno that last night when Carmen had finished packing her things and was waiting on her mom with a borrowed van. Juno sat on their bed looking at Carmen like she just knew she was leaving forever and when Carmen had leaned over to kiss her sweet little head goodbye, Juno had swiped her claws at Carmen and hissed before running under the bed.

"Come here," Carmen said to hedge-Juno. Carmen sat down on the bench and patted her legs invitingly, "Come here, sweet girl. I've missed you." Carmen's phone background used to be her, Sadie, and Juno cuddled in bed together some morning. She'd changed it when she moved but still opened her photo album to look at the picture from time to time. This Juno wasn't as cute with no whiskers and no mischievous eyes. No missing front tooth. Only the undergrown idea of a cat, really.

This Juno batted its paw in the air a few times and Carmen desperately tried to think of what to do. She eyed the long tendrils of new, greenish branches sprouting behind the creature, tying it to the bush it emerged from. Her fist automatically squeezed down around the garden shears.

"Can I leave, Juno? I've got to go," Carmen spoke to the cat. "You have to let me out of here. Okay?"

Hedge-Juno did not make any indication it had heard her. Carmen reached out with a shaking hand and touched the

—Eliza Marley—

cat-shaped-hedge on the top of its head. She stroked back the leaves there gently and the thing rustled under her touch.

Carmen reached out with the shears and cut the stem holding Juno to the rest of the hedge. They were not large enough to fully sever the link. The cat recoiled, its twiggy paws falling loose to the ground while all the bushes of the circle shook like they were rearing back on their haunches. Hedge-Sadie who had remained looming behind Juno darted, quicker than Carmen would have thought possible, to kneel in front of her, the creaking and snapping of reconfiguring branches echoing in the circle beside Carmen's ragged breath.

The thing was bracketing Carmen where she sat on the bench with its growing arms twisted around the bench legs. Carmen was reminded of how Sadie would get down next to her at the table and comb Carmen's hair back when she had been working too long. She would kneel and pet her thighs, sit on her lap as they watched TV. Pet her knee on the ride to work. Curl her nails around Carmen's neck and play with the hair at her nape. Sit across the table and watch her with a distant, cold gaze. Turn away when Carmen asked what was wrong. Give Carmen a look like she was the problem. This Sadie had the same expression, indented eyes boring down in a glare. Not giving her any room. Carmen wanted to push it. Yell at it. Hack at it with the garden shears.

"I miss you," Carmen said instead.

Hedge-Sadie's face turned up in some semblance of a sneer. Around them the bushes were still shaking, branches knocking against each other. When the creature breathed this time it sounded hoarse like it was clearing its throat.

—Eliza Marley—

"We could have worked things out," Carmen said. "You're always so dramatic. You wouldn't even talk to me."

The hedge creature opened its mouth and groaned, the sound of wood splintering. Branches snapping and leaves rapsing against each other erupted around them. As Carmen listened she thought back to the chatter of a cafe. Of cups clinking against metal patio tables.

The creature groaned in a low growling tone at her.

She and Sadie had been arguing more, every little thing one of them did seemed to irritate the other. They were going to bed at different times and on further edges of the bed. Sadie had been staying out more with friends and leaving Carmen to look after the apartment and the cat by herself. They were both broke and both too scared to apply to jobs outside their immediate area in case any change disrupted the last bubble of calm they both seemed to be clinging to.

At their normal brunch spot Carmen had gotten up to fetch their order from the counter. When she'd come back to the table Sadie was smiling up at some other girl who was leaning against their table talking to her. Sadie's hand on hers, fingers gently stroking.

Carmen didn't even know what they'd been saying. She was tired and on edge and holding both trays of food and drinks since Sadie hadn't even tried to get up and help her. Carmen had slammed the trays down, startling them both.

"Why are you such a slut?" She'd shouted at Sadie before she could stop it.

—Eliza Marley—

The other girl had frozen for a moment, staring up between Carmen and Sadie before murmuring something and running away. Carmen had watched her go. The whole patio had been silent, a crowd around them staring for a beat before awkwardly looking away and resuming their meals. Carmen's whole body had felt like a short circuited wire.

"You're not...I meant...I didn't mean..."she couldn't get a proper thought out. There was nothing else she'd meant to say. She just wanted to make Sadie feel for a moment as bad as she made Carmen feel all the time.

All Sadie had done was watch her silently, ice in her eyes and a practiced calmness pasted onto her face. Sadie had eaten her breakfast and left without saying a word to Carmen at all. She'd stayed at a friend's for a couple days with no contact before coming back home for 'the talk'. Replaying that scene over and over again, as Carmen had done numerous times in the last few weeks, Sadie hadn't even looked upset. Maybe even a little smug.

In the hedge circle the bushes continued their chatter, the noise roaring in Carmen's ears making her feel dizzy. Hedge-Sadie was still knelt in front of her offering no clear path of escape.

"I didn't mean it," Carmen yelled. "Like you never called me a name when you got mad? Like you never said anything mean? You didn't want to forgive me. You'd been waiting for a good enough excuse for months!"

Hedge-Sadie opened her mouth once more, "You... Slut..." it exhaled in a voice like splinters.

—Eliza Marley—

Carmen lunged. With the shears in hand, she closed them around as much of the creature's shoulder as she could, cutting a chunk free. The branches and trails of leaves that had wound together to make the body unraveled, leaving a lump of Hedge-Sadie on the ground as the rest of the creature hunched over to its side.

Tendrils of plant came pushing back out of the hedge walls to rebuild. Carmen reached out with the garden shears again, pushing herself back up as she cut off one of the branch arms winding itself towards her. "You are a self-centered asshole—" She snipped the shears again, chasing the appendage back towards the shrub it came from. "You always talked over me around our friends. You told everyone that story about me throwing up on the greyhound bus even though I asked you not to. You kept all of our cooking pans even though I bought them and I know you remembered that."

She cut into the hedge itself, worming the shears through the thick mass of growing leaves. "Stupid bushes," she grit out. "None of this matters anymore." She cut again and again, widening the gap. "I'm here now. It's all over."

Carmen felt her arm break through into open air. Without thinking she moved to push herself, head first, through the same hole, wiggling against the rough rasp of branches poking into her neck and shirt. Carmen winced against the pain of scraping twigs but dragged herself on, until she was standing outside the circle, back in the park's field.

Carmen caught her breath, patting herself down and feeling for any damage. She brushed some loose leaves out of her hair and felt for her phone and wallet, still in her pants

—Eliza Marley—

pockets. Her hand was on fire, the spot in between her pointer and thumb a bright red from squeezing down on the shears.

Turning back to the circle of hedges, she observed that it looked quite the same as before she had entered, with the addition of her escape gap and the bunch of severed twigs laying around it. Carmen walked carefully around the outside of the circle, hedge clippers still ready in her grip. The regular entrance had returned, leaving a clear opening into the bench circle. Another pile of twigs and leaves laid on the ground inside, perfectly innocuous. Carmen did not investigate further.

There was no sign of the gardener man so Carmen pocketed the shears and walked back across the field, past the park, the way she came. She straightened out her clothes as she went, smoothing down her short hair and retucking her shirt into her pants. She retraced her steps back to the bus stop she'd gotten off at. This block still had people out seated on patios, forks and plates clattering against metal tables. Carmen didn't bother to keep an eye out for the restaurant her coworkers were at.

The sun had set, leaving the sky a dark, dusty blue, offset by strands of light dangling between shops and the overhanging street lights. Carmen stood at the bus stop and waited. The shallow scrapes across her hand were an angry red. Carmen pressed her thumb against them and was relieved when they stung.

Across the street, a home goods store was still open. Its windows were full of assorted boxes. Coffee makers, rice cookers, blenders, and decorative oven mitts. A selection of small pots stood out to her. Clay and plastic that could hold a

—*Eliza Marley*—

small tomato plant or maybe some basil or even a cactus. Carmen left the bus stop and crossed the street, running against the light and ignoring the car that honked at her. A couple exiting the shop held the door for her and Carmen entered, wondering if they sold seeds to grow with the pots—and maybe a first aid kit as well.

—Eliza Marley (she/her)

—Eliza Marley—

The Witching Hour
—**Carella Keil** (she/her)

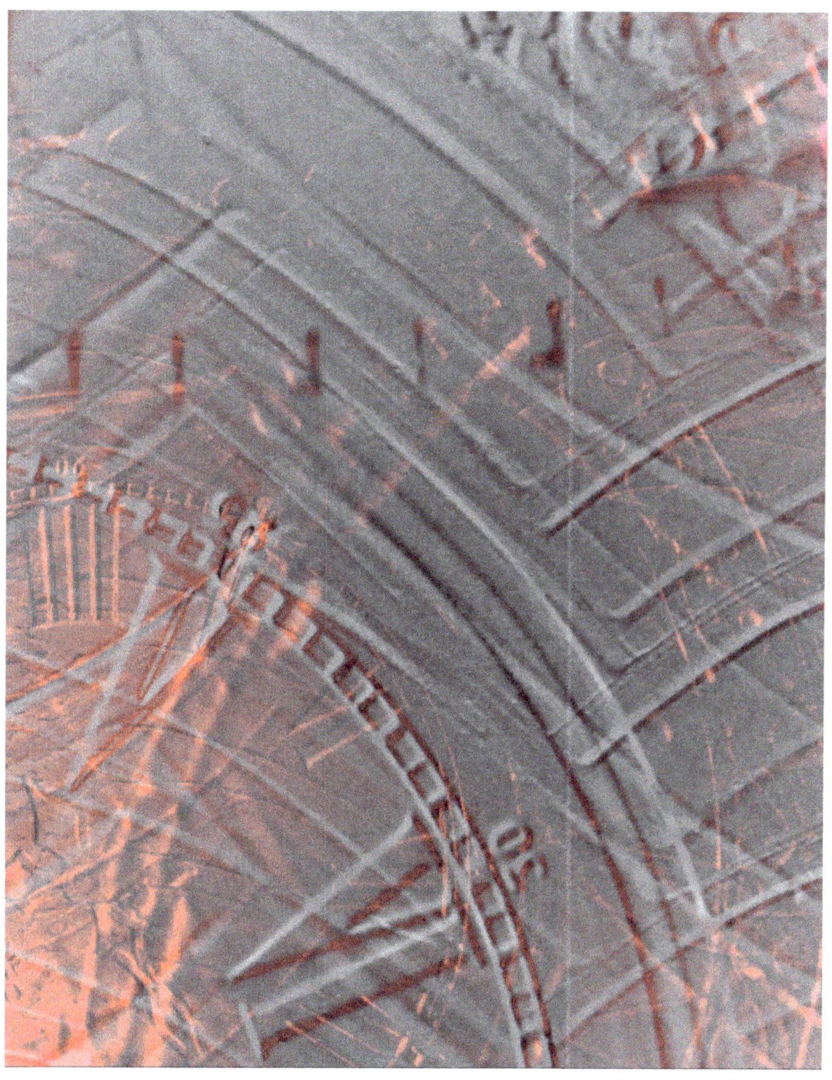

—Carella Keil—

Sacrificial: Loved and Damned

You are my shepherd and I
am your flock. Your fingers
delve into my white, ride
the waves. I nibble offerings
from your palms upheld
to the sun like a blessing.
You lead me, crooked cane
our companion, across rock
and meadow to streams
running clear as sandwich bags.
I drink. You watch and smile,
a waning crescent moon.
Your knife, a diamond star
in your back pocket, whispers
free. I lie in willow shade
that mimics dusk. "Sacrifice"
the leaves rustle and I suspend
my breath with knowledge.
You are my shepherd. I, your flock.

—Jennifer Ruth Jackson (she/her)

—Jennifer Ruth Jackson—

Notman

There's nothing like Whataburger after a night of drinking.

I don't know if it's the beer or the cooks or just how the world works, but a Whataburger grilled cheese at two in the morning is the most delicious thing on the planet. At least to me it is. Other folks say it's the burger or the patty melt but I've always been a sucker for the cheese. My mouth is watering just thinking about it by the time I pull in front of the drive-thru menu. There isn't a line tonight, luckily enough.

I wait a few seconds in front of the speaker, anticipating its staticky voice. A few seconds stretch into a minute. Someone should have taken my order by now, right? Whataburger is open 24 hours so I know there's someone on the line.

"Hellooo?" I call, trying to be as obnoxious as possible. No one answers. I'm a second away from calling it a night and giving Waffle House a shot when the speaker finally comes to life.

"Hel...lo? Wel...come?" says a strange voice, changing its tone and pitch with every syllable, as if trying out the words.

Fantastic. I've got a weirdo for a cashier. Sighing, I take a sip from my beer and lean towards the speaker so that they can better hear me.

"Yes, hello," I start slowly. "I'd like a grilled cheese please. That's it. Just one. Can you do that for me?"

The speaker is silent for a little while longer, because of course it is. I spoke too many words, probably. I tap the side of

—*Samuel Cooley*—

my car and take another sip while I wait on the worker to answer. An eternity later, their shifting voice returns.

"Come... get... it..."

"What's the price?" I ask. The voice hesitates again but I'm all out of patience. I just groan and drive towards the window, hoping the cashier can count better than they can talk.

There's no one there when I pull up. The inside is dark and there's a few drops of ketchup on the cash register, barely visible thanks to the outside light. The longer I stare the weirder it looks, so I move to the next window, ready to just grab my sandwich and call it a night.

A woman is waiting for me there. The same one answering the drive through, probably. After the fiasco at the speaker, I expected her to look a bit strange. A big head, a drooping face, something that shows why she talks the way she does. Instead, she's perfectly normal. She's got slightly chubby cheeks, dark brown hair, and blue eyes—though, those look off in a way I can't put my finger on.

She blinks slowly like a cat, and when she opens her eyes again I notice what's so strange about them. They look dry, like plastic. Eyes that would look more at home in a doll than a living, breathing person. It's hard to look away.

"Can... I... help you?" she asks, shifting her tone just like before until she decides on a high-pitched voice. It makes her sound like some preppy cheerleader.

"Yeah, just here for my sandwich," I say, feeling the alcohol fade out of me. Something is wrong. I don't know what—maybe it's the eyes or the voice or both—but I don't want

—Samuel Cooley—

to be here anymore. I ignore the feeling best I can. Soon I'll have my food and be back home drinking another beer, forgetting all about this. Just have to wait a little while longer is all.

"Right... the sandwich. Let me get that for you," she whispers. I watch her step away from the window and start walking towards the kitchen. On the way, she seems to see something behind the front counter, something just out of my sight, and stops to get a closer look. Of course she stops, heaven forbid she actually hurry for something. I look away to take another sip of beer—I need it at this point—and turn back to see that she's squatting now. Even her squats look weird, how can someone—

Her knees are bending the wrong way.

I can't help but shout a little. It's like she replaced her legs with a deer's, the knees bending backwards in a way no human's was ever meant to. In a blink, she's back at the window, leaning half her body out with a frown. Her dry eyes blink again, only a few inches in front of my own.

"Is something wrong?" she asks, all the tones from earlier combining at the final word. Something about that question seems off, like she's waiting for a special answer. Frantically, I shake my head.

"Sorry, sorry, didn't mean to scream. Thought I saw a cop. Not supposed to be driving, you know. That's all," I stammer out, holding up a can as proof. It's shaking. It needs to stop shaking. It needs to stop shaking now.

"Okay," she says before disappearing again. This time I wait until she's all the way in the kitchen to look away, breathing fast and hard as I stare at the wheel.

—Samuel Cooley—

Was that real? It couldn't have been. I'm too drunk. Way too drunk. Shouldn't even be driving. But I need to drive. I need to drive home right now. I need to slam my foot into the pedal and get as far away as possible. That thing isn't right. It isn't right, and if I don't drive home right this instant then it'll come for me.

My foot is already on the pedal when I stop myself. What am I thinking? I just admitted to someone that I'm drinking and driving. What if she hears me race off and calls the cops? I can't afford a lawyer. Not a good one. What am I supposed to tell the judge? Sorry, your honor, saw some weird knees and thought I'd speed across town.

I chuckle a bit, forcing my still shaking hands off the steering wheel. I'm being ridiculous. Had a bit more beer than I thought. That's all. I drop the almost empty beer can into my cup holder. No more for me. I'll go home, eat my food, and forget all about this in the morning.

"Your sandwich," the girl says, suddenly at the window. I turn, still chuckling, and see the bag she's holding out for me. My laughs stick in my throat.

The bag's soaked. Red is leaking out of the bottom in a steady drip, each drop splashing against the lip of the wall between us. If the girl notices something's off, she doesn't show it, she just keeps staring at me with those lifeless eyes.

Screw this.

My hands return to the steering wheel, gripping them like a lifeline while I try to slam my foot into the pedal. Like an idiot, I miss the damn thing and the girl, the thing, reaches forward and grabs my left arm before I can try again. The grip

—Samuel Cooley—

is tight enough to bruise, inhuman in its sudden strength, and I have to press the brake to keep my car from rolling on without me. The thing is still holding out the bag with its free hand, an offering yet to be taken.

"Is there something wrong?" it asks again, tilting its head.

"No, no," I stutter, trying to rip my arm away. It doesn't budge. "Nothing wrong at all. I love ketchup. Was just surprised."

"Sur...prise?" the thing asks, its head tilting further until the neck is almost at ninety degrees. It takes me a moment to realize that it is testing out a new word. It was learning. I was teaching the thing just by talking.

"Yeah," I whisper. "I really like the meal. I think it'll be good. Here, let me grab it."

It still doesn't release its grip. I have to reach over with my right hand, tangling our limbs together to grab the soaked bag. When I finally have it in my hand, I throw it into the seat next to me like it's something rotten.

"Thanks for the meal," I say, feeling the tears build up behind my eyes. I can't cry now. Not yet. Later I can cry and wail and scream until I can make sense of what's happening, but right now I need to leave. Need to drive and keep on driving until there is nothing in sight.

"Eat it."

"What?" I ask, wincing as the grip somehow tightens.

—Samuel Cooley—

"You like it. Eat it. Is there something wrong?" it asks, lips slowly turning up into a smile. It's mocking me. A predator playing with its food.

I can't help the tear that slides down my cheek. I reach over and open up the bag, pulling out the mess of a meal inside. It's a sandwich, exactly what I ordered, but the bread is soaked with a thick red liquid. I know what it is but I can't say it. I can't think it. But I can smell it. I can smell it and I know what it is and I can't do anything about it. I take a bite.

The red liquid leaks out of the bread as soon as I bite down, drowning the other flavors of the sandwich. It clogs my throat and sticks to my tongue as I chew. I almost vomit immediately, but I manage to swallow the first bite somehow. I can't do it again. I can't. I'll break and cough or vomit and it'll know something is off. It'll know I know. What then? What will it do to me then?

I don't have to answer. The grip on my arm releases and I almost collapse into the wheel in relief. I glance over to see if I fooled the thing but I wish I hadn't. It isn't smiling anymore, it's grinning. It's grinning with too many rows of teeth, some sharp, some blunt, and none of them remotely human.

"Thanks for the meal," it says in my voice. My voice. I can't help it, I scream. I barely notice the thing's smile drop as I drop the sandwich and slam on the gas pedal, not missing this time . My tires squeal, keeping me there just long enough to see the thing open its mouth wide, too wide, and cry out the most repulsive sound I've ever heard. Like a tornado siren combined with grinding metal.

—Samuel Cooley—

The thing is too late though, I'm already driving. It leaps out the window, legs bending at the same strange angle, but it's nowhere near as fast as a car, not even when it gets down on all fours. I can see it bend and contort in my back window, chasing me down with that same horrific screech, but there's nothing it can do now.

I don't let up the gas for a second, even after it fades from sight. A few other vehicles honk their horns as I speed down the road but it doesn't matter. They can honk all they want. I escaped, I escaped, I escaped!

I'm not driving for long before the smell hits me. The bag from earlier is still sitting in my car, staining the seats with a rotten stench. I pull over immediately and stumble out of car, vomiting more food and drink than I can remember eating. It's red. Oh God, it's red.

I reach into the car and grab the bag, throwing it as far as I can. Away from me, away from my car, away from anything normal. Then I finally cry. I cry like I haven't since I was a baby. It makes my legs too weak to hold me and my body too useless to do anything but shake.

I don't know how long I stay sobbing in a ball as cars pass by. I just know I can't stop. It might have been minutes or it might have been hours until the tears finally dry and the sobs quiet. I am about to stand up and walk back to my car when something grabs my shoulders in a tight, familiar grip. Something's breath trickles down my spine.

It's not real, it's not real, it's not real. Nothing's wrong. It's—

—*Samuel Cooley*—

"Surprise," my voice whispers behind me. I don't know which one of us screams.

—Samuel Cooley (he/him)

—Samuel Cooley—

The Body

Moss devours unmarked gravestones, an incomplete twinning of calves I watched perish in the hay.

A withering shadow discards the remains of a young woman in the woodlands, her body floating in the faraway creek, a newfound surface for flowers to grow, their rigid stems sprouting from a curved spine.

We find her lying face down beneath the ice, the creek frozen, an animal's scratch marks etched against the frost, strands of dark hair slithering through a crack, an abandoned feast.

Her fatty tissue could be used as soap. I imagine rubbing her against my skin, savoring her marshmallow scent until my hair is yanked in the shower by a hidden specter.

We're forced to become nocturnal, a gathering of skittish mice who remain motionless in the presence of slow footsteps stalking our hallway, a darkness standing outside our doors, shielding slivers of protective light.

I wake up, a strong smell of mildew rising from beneath my bed. Delicate curtains hover in the morning's gentle wind, a satiated fog beginning to dissipate.

I watch an unknown man leave our garden carrying a briefcase, his suit wrinkled, an instant decision to finally replace the broken padlock.

—**Chimen Georgette Kouri** (she/her)

—Chimen Georgette Kouri—

Spawn

A sharp pain deep in my abdomen took the breath right out of my lungs, causing me to double over in front of the restaurant cashier. She barely cocked an eyebrow as she continued inputting the burger combo I had just ordered on the register.

"Did you want cheese on that?" she asked, voice just as uninterested as her expression. I struggled for a moment to catch my breath.

"Uh, yeah, sure," I said, rubbing my lower stomach in an attempt to calm the discomfort. I passed her a crumpled $10 bill and told her to keep the change.

"For here?" she asked. "To go," I replied.

"We'll bring it out to you when it's ready."

She handed me a number, giving me the cue to awkwardly shuffle away. I felt lightheaded but found a seat to wait for my order. My mouth was dry, I regretted not adding a drink.

Pressure built in my gut until I had to muffle a burp. I wrote the sudden uncomfortable sensation off as a bad batch of gas from my empty stomach, but the escaping air didn't cause the feeling to ease up. I looked down to find myself lightly bloated, which wasn't too odd for me, but still, I furrowed my brow. Had I looked like that all day?

Undoing the button on the fly of my jeans provided some relief, as did slumping across the table with my cheek resting on the cold surface. I stuck slightly to the table, but chose to bury

—Vix Martin—

my disgust by taking slow, calculated breaths.

I was exhausted even though my day at work had gone pretty smoothly—I had woken up tired, despite not really staying up all too late, and I hadn't slept badly. Well, there had been a dream that had shot me up in bed covered in a cold sweat, but when I tried to remember it I could only conjure quick flashes; a feeling of damp heat, colors that swirled together in swaths of blue, purple, and yellow, and an intense, overwhelming *feeling* that I couldn't describe. Attempting to put it into words while panting in my bed had reduced me to tears. Like any odd dream, the imagined tension quickly dissipated as I sat in my real bed, covered by my real blanket, staring at my apartment closet with the sliding door that was always slightly off the track no matter what I did.

Dreams didn't usually stay with me like that; I felt a familiar chill down my spine.

"34?" A tall teenage boy called out as he lifted the door in the counter to bring out a greasy bag. Grabbing the number tent, I raised my hand up off the table.

"I'm here," I said, not bothering to lift my head.

He delivered the bag, but forgot to take my number. "Oh hey man, you forgot this."

I took the plastic table tent and gestured in his direction with it, half-sitting up in the process. He turned back to me, giving me a good look at his own tired face and to my surprise, a bloated stomach that seemed even more distinct on his tall, wiry frame. A sheen of sweat covered his pale, clammy face.

"You feeling okay?" I asked, pulling my hand back from

—Vix Martin—

him.

"A little tired," he said dismissively.

I watched him stumble his way back into the kitchen, bumping into the gate with a wince and a whispered "Goddammit." Nothing had seemed off to me when I first came in, but now that I was looking around I noticed similar symptoms in just about everyone. One woman that my brain had categorized as simply being pregnant looked particularly off. She sat slumped in a rear booth, legs spread haphazardly as she panted, sweat now visibly streaming down her brow.

Her abdomen was so distended that it looked like she wouldn't have been able to stand up from the booth without considerable effort. Food was going ignored, half-eaten on her dine-in tray as she panted, putting both hands on her stomach, applying pressure.

I could have sworn I saw her belly shudder.

Anxiety quickly gave way to fear in my mind as I glanced down at my own body just to see my own growth had doubled in size. A feeling of panic washed over me, chilling me, but I was unable to translate the feeling in any meaningful way, instead simply reaching into my bag to grab a fry while they were still fresh and warm.

The cashier collapsed behind the register with a discordant clatter as she knocked the drawer from the till.

I ate another fry. Man, they were really good today.

A sickening sound from the woman furthest along filled the restaurant; a wet mix of a sharp tear, a choked scream, and a thick plop that dissolved into flopping slaps on the white tile.

—Vix Martin—

Thick, slug-like creatures had torn through the woman's flesh to gush out in a burst of sudden activity. They slunk across the ground as I stared with dead eyes in their direction, similar to how the cashier had looked at me.

Blood thickened with black ichor inched its way out from her twitching corpse. Bits of flesh clung to the creatures as they began to feel their way back towards her fading body heat. The viscera sank into the writhing slugs, melting slowly into their bodies. Trails opened up through the sea of dark, off-colored blood in their wakes as they inched gracelessly back to their source.

Another burst of fluids and life exploded behind the counter as the girl succumbed to the pressure as well, allowing the wet creatures to spread into the kitchen. The food runner slipped in the mess, shoes making a sharp squeak when his foggy mind wouldn't allow him to react in time to keep himself from falling. His skull cracked sharply against the counter on his way down.

People continued to move through the motions of ordering food even as no one took note until they too had all sunk into booths or onto the floor if no seat was available near them.

The table was pushing down on my stomach as I tried to shift in my seat, pinning me in place. The pressure allowed me to feel writhing life growing rapidly just below the surface, twisting together in a gut-churning knot as it shifted my organs out of its impatient, demanding way.

Flashes of light similar to the ones in my dream blinded me, but I couldn't be sure if they were a memory or something

—Vix Martin—

actually happening.

The doors pushed open to allow a pair of people inside, both leaning on the handles under the weight of their own bodies combined with their invasive new inhabitants before sinking to the ground. One of them had their head resting on the other's chest for a front row seat to the gush of blood and other fluids as the amorphous creatures fought their way free, only to seek out the other's slack mouth to force their way inside, initiating another expulsion.

I turned my attention back to the first woman to pop to find her body covered by the undulating mass she had birthed, each leaving a trail of digested, exposed flesh in its wake as they inched their way across her body.

A stabbing pain resonated from near my belly button, stronger than the now constant throbbing of activity within me. The pain bloomed white-hot as the first tentacle tore its way free.

The pain was excruciating as I split open, spilling viscera along with the new life, mixed with sludge that shone like motor oil in the light. The lights swung overhead as something passed by over the building, shaking the foundation as it hovered momentarily. The vibrations allowed me to slide out of the booth, crashing to the ground in the puddle of meat and fluids that had once been me.

I saw yellow, blue, and purple lights flashing in a cycle outside as the freshly born things began to cover my body. The ability to scream was only granted back to my body as my mouth was spread wide around a living intrusion that was seeping digestive juices over my skin, sinking deep into the soft flesh of

—Vix Martin—

my mouth, dissolving it for the creature to then absorb through its putrid being.

—**Vix Martin** (they/them/fae/faer)

—*Vix Martin*—

Ingrid M. Calderón-Collins (she/her)

—Ingrid M. Calderón-Collins—

The Compost

Creating life is difficult. I find it best to start with my hands.

Years ago, when I was first allowed into my father's office (it took a while to get there due to my limbs being an inappropriate size and my childhood clumsiness not having yet vanished), I discovered that he had a large shelf of untouched books; The biology department he led nobly had outgrown the molded books from the early parts of the decade. So I touched them, excitedly. One level at a time.

I remember feeling his eyes peer over his gold-rimmed glasses, watching me with a careful frown.

I flinched and pulled away my fingers once I touched a novel with wet mildew.

Incredibly, it had pussed and pooled out from underneath its papers, staining its siblings on the shelf along with the wood.

"You can take one," He gruffed from behind his desk. "But I expect it back."

The delight I had from hearing my father not only choose to forfeit the strict material of the gift, but to increase its value by allowing it to be selected by my hands, would have made me the happiest child alive if my happiness had not been eclipsed by a storm of worry clouding over my face. Suddenly, I felt unworthy to be the chooser of my own gift. How ungrateful and spoiled I was to even think I could make the correct call. I slumped to the ground, overwhelmed by the weight of my father's kindness and fell into the sound of his sighs. Fleeting patience, breathing in and out.

—Sarah Kuntz—

I turned my head to the lower shelf. A copper-colored spine caught my attention. "What is—" I turned my head, reading it sideways, "—composting?"

I waited on the ground for an answer. In the visible crack between the floor and the desk, I watched my father's feet swivel themselves to the farthest wall, cramming his body into the corner until his left ankle got itchy and he lifted the pant leg with his right foot. With the pointed end of his loafer, he stabbed the itch aggressively, scratching the exposed skin above his black sock. When finished, he stopped and shuffled some papers above, tapping his fingers on the briefcase to a mindless, far away tune.

My eyes traveled back to the copper spine; I prayed to the universe that the book would be in a good enough condition to be read. Luck had sprung from my fingers as I pulled it out from the shelf and witnessed a faded picture of colorful mud; pockets of dirt and various debris souped together in a large pot. Above it, read a title: *The Wonders of Composting: Feeding All Around You.* Opening it released a smell of moths and still water. Time had stained the first couple of pages and I read them vigorously. Though the compost and I had to eventually part, my mind and future were not vacant of it.

"Feed everything," I whispered, excited to finally experience my first harvest. The child-like joy, shaking inside my adult fingers. "Feed them. All the time."

My little town grew from the oath I had made with the book.

Early in winter was when it needed to be prepared, though the grateful earth wouldn't feel the plunders till spring.

—Sarah Kuntz—

I needed time to collect the corrected elements and get the recipe right before mixing it with precious soil; The worms I had plucked from the massacring rain had agreed. The dirt was divine.

Tirelessly, I mended my compost pile. Though it started in an old wheelbarrow found eroding in an empty lot, I noticed the heap had quickly overrun the rusted borders and threatened to flow past the oilless wheels. It became clear to me: I needed to expand. The infant pile surpassed next week's wooden solutions and moved far beyond the inflexible porcelain of an abandoned clawfoot tub.

Soon, there was no choice but the barren barn itself.

The sunbeams that cascaded in from the silo's high windows now welcomed the fumes sailing up from the dying fruits, granting them life through manifested rot. A phantom made from the smells winked at me and wished me safe travels on my journey back home. While locking up for the night, I shut the doors with the last scrap of strength left for me on the day's timetable with the hope that this would all be enough for the soil. Enough for the compost to marry.

Good fortune for my stand tripled as they became aware of my natural creations. My crops had become responsible for every squash and rutabaga-based meal. Every husked corn and soft potato served endlessly in autumn's kitchen, shared by an odiferous breeze blowing in and throughout the town.

The demand for my food quickly soured the blessing and I had lost most of my compost.

Before next Saturday, when most of my crops would sell at the local farmer's market, I needed to make haste with the

—Sarah Kuntz—

leftover mixture I had. At the end of my evening, I realized that I wouldn't have enough to start the crops for next season, let alone support the existing seeds, wilted and hungry for only the purified and Frankenstein fertilizer living here in my barn. I began to panic, watching twilight embers burn into the night's fire until I saw the moon project the most devious of plans.

I fastened my cloak and carried my lantern down the untraveled road that led straight to the backwoods behind my barn, and made sure that tonight, I would not be a chicken. I'd keep bravery close to the chest.

As I crept by the neighboring homes, hidden behind bare and black trees, I saw a dim light in the distance. Following it, I found a family, sitting at a table, eating my harvest.

Quietly, I slipped closer, and in my attempt to get a better look, I knocked over their garbage pail. The loudness of the crash made their heads turn toward the window. I darted back into the darkness and shivered there, hiding in midnight's comforting arms. Embarrassed, I realized I had spooked myself.

"It's a scavenger," I read the mother's lips while she comforted the kids. "Nothing to be frightened of."

Guilt and doubt swept over me in waves: *What am I doing?* And my thoughts began to threaten me with the promise of no crops, which meant no food would be present at my stand.

Conflicted, I began to clean up their waste.

In my hands lay scattered coffee grounds that practically spelled out the solution: I needed to diversify the food in my heap if I wanted a more prosperous, more time-controlled feast.

—Sarah Kuntz—

While my reason looked the other way, I pocketed the coffee along with some of its friends.

I woke up the next morning with early thoughts of failure, but those cleared away the minute my arms swung open the barn doors and I could smell the pleasant decay from where I stood.

There, in the middle of the pond-sized pile, I spotted the various treasures I had stolen from my neighbor. Splendidly, the coffee grounds, a dozen eggshells, and an herbed tea bag, turned beige from the soaked chamomile inside, had not only enmeshed themselves with the old compost but had coaxed more worms to migrate toward the center (an issue I had not been able to remedy previously due to the shyness of the colonies). Now they left casings needed for the soil.

Smiling, I listened to the sounds of their chewing, and whether imaginary or not, I let the noise occupy all my senses. A vision of their toothless gums devouring my pile filled my eyes and I swore I heard singing. A choir of worms, growing full and fast.

After their feasting, I replenished my crops with this new, casing-rich compost. In the weeks after, my stalks, bushels, and dwarf trees had matured into beautiful gents of the garden; new ladies were now able to wave at the male plants with twirling leaves from a fresh pumpkin's vine. I was rich with monstrous vegetation of frightening size and it chilled my spine with immense happiness knowing all of the hungry mouths that could be easily fed.

As I harvested them, I heard a small banging in the distance. I looked up at the horizon to the little hill where my

—Sarah Kuntz—

barn stood and found the doors had released themselves from their lock—the padlock lay dangling to the side like a person with something green, hanging down from their teeth.

In the wind, the doors flapped wildly, letting anyone see inside the barn's chambers. Though impossible, it was smiling and trying to gain my attention; harmonizing with the whistling sounds of the wind, I could hear its wooden mouth scream, "Look, Papa! Look how good I've done!" And although alarmed, I had no choice but to wave back to my son and brighten my face. Show off the pride, beaming.

Dangerously, mine and my compost's desires had become entwined. We had both grown accustomed to these new, enriched ingredients and were unprepared to go back to our old citrus-ring-ways, nor were we satisfied with stale bread from the kitchen. No, the waste we wanted, more or less demanded, was out there waiting for us in the town's forgotten, living patiently for a mycelium death.

But wasn't I also a promising reaper? I asked myself. *Wouldn't I be granted the chance to steal the fruits, wasted by the town, if it meant that what was stolen would be delivered to that same owner's mouth? Would it be unethical, unregulated farming, to zombify old scraps? To give them new life?*

All my questions were worthless compared to my bigger motivation; no longer was it just worms occupying my compost. Now I had roly-polys from out of town and black soldier flies who stayed and promised me their larvae burrowing their future lives down in my heap. And if those guests weren't enough, the bugs and I were gifted a lone, little-legged spider. At first, we welcomed the creature with caution, knowing that spiders were traditionally predators, but soon, the spider had joined in on the

—Sarah Kuntz—

symbiotic composting. And my pile altered the spider's appetite. As it feasted on the same waste as its insectoid friends I eventually began to wonder: who or what could be invited?

It was solidified as it was certain: an afternoon spent with the full bug jamboree forced me to leave all my old, botanical senses and go searching for a new understanding, deep in the night.

Unfortunately, when it came time, I had been a day late for the garbage.

With wilted faith, I watched as the garbage truck rolled down the way, taking with it all my glorious plans for the town. Yet, the truck's mouth seemed too small to fit every waste option. I thought eagerly of dumpsters, sitting behind the town's grocery marts, the general store, and the busy-by-day docks down on Harbor Street. Swiftly, I scored some newfound treats: used napkins with the corners torn and chewed off from a rat I had fought in the alley, expired crab and kelp meal from a sleeping fisherman's cooler, and a goopy eye, falling off the molten face of a cooked goose, burned and thrown out to the gutters. All of them went with me back to the woods.

I snickered quietly, quite proud of myself and my general sagacity. And the backwoods had their own gifts for the compost. I fell on all fours, bringing my face close to their treasures, afraid to miss them.

After pulling live roots from the earth, my hands had cracked sodded clumps in search of maggots or hungry beetles, I had found a greater prize: a dead rabbit lay limp in my arms as I cradled its chest up to my ear, making sure it wouldn't bounce up in surprise. Carefully, I collected the rabbit with the rest of

—Sarah Kuntz—

my findings and it was as if the small critter had unlocked a new level of macabre. My hands trailed behind me, catching every leftover nest with dead and abandoned baby birds. My face glowed with excitement when it realized that I had unattached antlers from the sunken head of a deceased deer.

By the time I had reached the barn, I was congratulating myself. Buoyed by my success, I dropped all the death on the pile and went right back into town. Dawn was approaching, and I had just enough time. It was not too late to amplify my cleverness to a higher degree.

I stood in front of cemetery gates with a shovel in my hands. I did not leave till I was covered in boney dirt, the sun being able to painfully shine itself in my eyes. I had what I needed.

Days later, I reared myself to open the barn doors, nervous to see how the investment developed. Wonderfully, the compost had changed to a darkened delight. The material of the compost, though I had witnessed it wet before, had progressed to a level of sponged moisture mimicking a soft mattress. Soiled plushness that tempted me into an insistent hug. And together, without the weight of shame, we embraced each other and our newfound greatness. Around my snow-angeling arms, smaller bugs traveled on the back of worms, ready to greet me, and the larger and more built creatures pushed the bones from the cemetery like a canoe entering the still waters of a lake. Elbows and knees carried expectant mothers filled with flies and a large skull toppled over, flinging a family of spiders down into the pile's sea. I opened my palm, bringing them up to my cheek, and let them kiss me. The message was clear—peace had finally

—Sarah Kuntz—

found us. The compost was beyond perfect. We would have plenty to harvest in whatever season we pleased.

But, like a mother not ready for their child's first day of school, I struggled to release my figure from its soft body and resist its pooling, loosening, and attempted escape.

My compost was stronger than I realized. Instead of bucking me off like a wild horse, it carried me and the other bugs straight to the door. I interrupted its departure from the barn by quickly kicking it closed with my left boot, and as expected, the pile was angry.

I stared at the exit, begging myself to stay calm and not lash out at the precious heap, reminding myself that the compost didn't mean to stomp, and it didn't actually want me and the vibrant community that had sprouted upon its rootless earth to leave it now.

Yet, continuously, I watched the compost slither up to the door, pounding on it with a determined pace. Cries for help traveled through clouds of rotten smoke, bursting in the air, releasing a terrible, stenchful scream, calling to be released.

The collective panic I saw on the bugs' faces was far worse than the compost's betrayal. Bravely, I extended out my arms and allowed them all to climb on top of my body and use me as a lifeboat. I whispered reassurance to them, promising them that the compost would stop and they'd be alright. But the bugs became restlessly frightened and they began to crawl up to my face, itching a terrible scratch over both of my closed eyes.

I opened them and found empty sockets.

—Sarah Kuntz—

Deeper my fingers went, trying to retrieve what I believed had fallen back into my brain, but found nothing. Though miraculously I could still see, and the sight frightened me so: my fingers were stripped of their flesh and were barely bendable. Like wet twigs.

I looked down my torso and silently smiled. My bugs were still here! And not only that, they continued to eat on the compost. I felt dried tears on my face as if I had already cycled through happiness and felt grateful for their long-time devotion to me and the rest of the town's soil. Hunger-driven, they seemed famished.

I lay in the compost, content in staring at the wooden door, listening to their chewing, until I noticed it.

The compost had broken off the handle and it appeared that the door was an angular, oddly shaped plank. Its size alone was just big enough for my body to walk through.

Curious, I tried to push on it and felt ill when it did not budge—I felt movement above me. Someone walking on my roof.

No matter what, I thought, shaking, *I'll just stay here, happy in my compost.*

And so I did. Though truthfully, I couldn't just lie there with work still to be done. And the bugs worked tirelessly. I was so proud of their ability to find nourishing food, though it brought me shame not being able to be their deliverer. But I found another way to be useful: I emotionally supported the spiders, flies, and worms whenever they needed a push in the right direction. I made tunnels with my fleshless fingers and

—Sarah Kuntz—

sang loudly over the crying voices, talking over the funeral march, just to ease them from knowing of the world above.

It was not our choice to be symbiotic; it was needed if we wanted to feed everything, all the time.

—**Sarah Kuntz** (they/them)

—Sarah Kuntz—

Dawn of the Dead 1:25

<u>Patient Interest Questionnaire</u>

Form must be completed in full and returned to gender regulators so that they may assist you in ensuring you are abiding to cisheteronormative ordinances.

Name: <u>Like undelivered letters, Trans and Gender Non-Conforming folx are post-</u>

Date: <u>marked as liminal spaces. We're caught between the living and dead like cell</u>

Age: <u>membranes blebbing—a programmed death. Society regulates bodies placing</u>

Email Address: <u>constraints upon us like a contagion, fear pushing them to keep ot—</u>

Phone Number: <u>hers from slowly rotting into the (un)dead like overripe bananas.</u>

—**Joel Sedano** (they/them)

—Joel Sedano—

Where The Wild Horses Cry

At the end of a small town in the garden state laid a worn down home and a thousand graves, which had never been found or touched. This is why we must never trust our mothers.

Autumns were exceptional and quiet up north for the vast and ever-growing, and dying, ecosystem. The cemeteries looked that way too, only unkempt. Ffion felt indebted to the spirits at the graveyard; discarding trash, raking the leaves, picking at the ingrown nails on her fingers, leaving her offerings where she stood. Gutting the chicken down to the bone and grinding the meat till she was able to toss it in with vegetables from the harvest. *The spirits liked it dirty.* Tinctures touched her blood-sore lips as she folded the pie into the pan and threw it in the oven. She eyed the staircase to see if her mother had come home.

"She'll show up eventually," whispering to herself.

As she brought the pie to the graveyard she nodded at the nearby crows flying in her direction.

November was starting soon, and that meant there would be an uprise in crows. They would soon commence their death dance, where they would gather in the trees and sing. It was almost haunting how you could spot them. They look at you with their black eyes like they absorbed your secrets. The murder of crows never hesitated to follow her home and sit on her decaying, rusted roof.

Ffion dropped some coins for the keeper. He was a large man carved into the stone with a dog by his side.

—*Cypress Wilde*—

Ffion's bedroom looked directly out to a field which proved to always be up to something unseen at night. She woke in a surge of terror from her nightmare, hearing something like a horse's cry. In the outstretched landscape, appeared a blurry, shadowy, mist-like figure with red luminescent eyes. She felt bugs crawling down her crooked spine, and turning with her lantern in hand, there was nothing except darkness. She had seen them once before, only in a trance. *The gwyllgi.* The hellhound of the night. An omen of death. Not a dog one wants to see it in the middle of the night. The gwyllgi was a hound from Cymru that had often represented death and madness. He was black with eyes glowing crimson. According to folklore, he stops someone dead in their tracks, it's worse to see him at the crossroads during twilight. He's known to paralyze them with their fear as they die.

In the bathroom mirror she looked at herself and shuddered. Clumps of faint strawberry hair were falling out with dead skin cells attached, a swollen infected jaw, rotting teeth, dark bags dragged down her eyes in an uncanny way. Ffion started plucking her eyebrows and scratching her face, thinking of her mother.

Her nails went back and forth across her skin until red lines appeared and the spidery veins came flushing to the surface. *I hate you I hate you I hate you I hate you I hate you I hate you I hate you I hate you.*

Deep scars laid on her body from her skull to her feet and she was missing all her eyelashes on one eye and a good portion of her scalp was cleared out like a corn field. Ffion scraped her body clean until it was irritated enough she could shock herself with ice. She looked more grotesque than she did

—Cypress Wilde—

before. But she no longer looked like her mother.

Her bloodshot eyes took a turn and settled on the figure at the back of the kitchen to the garden. It stood there, drooping arms and piercing white eyes. Their mouth was gaping open like a dog bite, flesh flowing to the ground. Another spirit—one she could not remember the name of. Another entity for her to take care of. She laid on the ground and opened her arms as if it would embrace her.

Nothing.

Ffion crawled to a cabinet near the basement and pulled out a dropper bottle filled with belladonna. Venetian women used it to make themselves look doe-like. The extract would dilate their pupils and make them more appealing to men. But if one took too much, it was said to cause madness. While she didn't know what she was doing, she placed three drops in each eye. After about thirty minutes it began to set in—she looked over at the entity sitting on her couch, weathered down by years of use.

"Can we talk?" It turned its head to face her—the unnamed entity didn't really care for the girl. It went on its way, but she continued. She was always lonely.

Her deep breathing settled in the center of her cardiac cage, tears streaming to the surface, making her throat burn.

No one likes me, not even the dead.

She laid there, almost lifeless, watching the ceiling lights flicker with her bambi eyes while she effortlessly licked the blood off her hands and dug her nails into the carpet.

Her breath shook as she took her fingers softly out of her mouth; her heart was beating so fast that there began a

—Cypress Wilde—

constant pool of red leaking out of her mouth. There in her palm laid a molar and a canine, which fell apart like mush as she rolled them between her fingers. Pulling it out *felt good* to her. She watched the blood drip, her jaw exhaling and reconstructing, a wound up animal. The wind rustled in the trees, mountains of red and yellow covered the horizon. The air smelled like molding pumpkins and magic. The foxes came to collect her offerings.

"Harvest season, time for giving," she told herself as she tore parts of her body away for the spirits. Their eyes called to her, pupils dark like the abyssal sea and mouths filled with sharp teeth.

"I must bring them something else tomorrow."

something something something something something
something something something something something
something something something something something
something something something something something
something something something something something
something something something something something
something something something something something
something something something something something
something something something something something
something something something something something
something something something something something
something something something something something
something something something something something
something something something something something

—Cypress Wilde—

something something something something something
something something something something something
something something something something something
something something something something something
something something something something something
something something something something something
something something something something something
something something something something something

Her words scrambled as the iron taste swarmed her mouth like maggots to a dead deer. The animals could barely understand her. *If they wish for more teeth I'll rip them all out until my mouth is nothing but holes.* She already enjoyed licking her lips and pushing her tongue in and out of them. The sensation gave her something to focus on other than pulling off her skin.

Her body cascaded around the dark trees as she turned onto her street. The old broken house waited for her as if it was a lost child.

Go start the fire. Go shower. Turn the lanterns off, then sleep. Sleep.

She rushed awake with the sudden urge to cry. The wail of the wild horses made her ears explode.

The graves that day were fighting the mud from the rain, but as she laid down each bouquet, the sun rose from the clouds like the gods themselves had heard her. She took her brush and lightly cleaned each stone, paying careful attention to the ones that were eroding. She made sure to bring coins to the

—Cypress Wilde—

guardian, tipping him nicely for his protection efforts. Sitting under the pine tree, she spun her hair in her hands and watched the sun rise, pastel like cotton candy. One of the only treats her mother let her have at the local carnivals in late July. It helped with the early decay of her beautiful sharp white teeth. She couldn't stop eating until someone dragged her away.

Her mind and vision was filled with screams and contorted uncanny faces.

The horses were returning.

Her hands clung to the kitchen cabinet as she stuffed the stems of the precious pink foxglove into her mouth and chewed violently while choking on the harsh stems. A headache immediately started to swell in the temples of her face, leaving her speechless. The pink flowers went down the easiest, they were soft and delicate, innocent perhaps. They didn't know they would be her demise. Something began to touch Ffion's head while she spun around her kitchen. The dishes had been piling up for weeks, rats rummaged through the feces and dirt, looking for any ounce of something edible. Lugging her body upstairs, she laid on her bed as if in a trance.

What her mother had done all those years never made her life easier like she had promised. She had abandoned her the minute that she desired more, better. Because *what is a mother's love if not true? How could it be true if it hurt so much? If it made me into a monster?*

"I am your mother and I know what's best. God will love us more

—Cypress Wilde—

now. They all love their offerings." her words twisted like strung organs on a willow tree.

Ffion mumbled under her breath. "You don't know anything."

I'm going to die alone and be alone forever. I never got to accomplish anything. I see it clearly now, she killed my spirit. And I killed the vessel. I killed the vessel. The vessel. Vessel. The. I killed the vessel. But I don't wish to be alone.

The foxglove began crumbling her insides, she had been violently puking for hours, her heartbeat slowed, and her breathing became jagged. Cold sweats began radiating down her in slow motion. Death knows no master.

She found death's kiss in a goddess with long flowing orange hair. Where The Wild Horses Sing. At the edge of the cliffs of Cymru

—Cypress Wilde (they/them)

—Cypress Wilde—

Bolton Leather Belt

No longer available in stores.

Hand-tooled genuine black calf-leather oiled to a fine sheen
for maximum flexibility of movement. Quarter-inch
thickness provides heft and sturdy grip. Your child
will never forget the clatter of the burnished silver
buckle when you remove this belt.
This belt can be stripped from the loops of khaki trousers
heavy denim or god-awful corduroys
with a satisfying *thwick* that will set your four-year-old
a-trembling. You may have to hold her wrists.
In public this belt efficiently bears weight
and cuts a clean silhouette when you
tuck in your church shirt. In private
this belt tightens up loose behavior.
Does your child squirm during the Sunday sermon?
Does your child look around too much? Start to
fall asleep? Cry a little bit? Ask wide-eyed
questions in a lisped whisper? Walk her out
the church door, marching double-time. Break out
this hand-tooled black calf-leather belt
in the back of the minivan. When your child
calls for her mother, remind her that Mommy
can't hear her. And if your child sobs that she is sorry,
flex your fingers around this thick, serviceable strap.
Let the buckle rattle.
And if your child flinches, remind her:
it will hurt worse if you hit her back or her legs.
Let her shiver a little before you start to count the lashes.

—Sophie Farthing—

And if your child pees all over you from pure fear
in her itchy red Christmas tights,
warm piss soaking into your corduroys,
wrap your hand around this flexible strap of masculine
calfskin and remind yourself that next time,
you gotta take the kid to the bathroom
before you get out the belt.

—**Sophie Farthing** (she/her)

—Sophie Farthing—

The Little Monster

Limbs stitched together with a crimson thread
before you lay it back upon a
walnut Rococo bed, a girl gone dead
nonconsensually revived, yesterday,
a resurrected bride. Its brain dispatched
of memories—the convulsive thuds
of murdered trees she once wandered past,
unable to save, before they drained her blood
to feed a grave. Fairest flesh, you would not waste.
Electrodes upon an eroding face
which tastes the lightning until a heart will race
becoming sentient, for you, posthaste
though neither chaste nor human by design,
a little monster ready by bedtime.

—**Kristin Garth** (she/her)

—Kristin Garth—

Soulace

—**Carella Keil** (she/her)

**Originally published in Margins Magazine Vol. 4 Issue 5*

—Carella Keil—

You Can't Let it Sting You

"Wait…Where did it go? You can't let it sting you!" Deven strains. After a day of taking off sun goggles to look directly into the planet's fourth sun and climbing encompassing forest trees with cyan leaves the size of cars, why did Deven have to dare her sister to catch that wasp? The same rare, tangerine-and-magenta-striped wasp that had flown from their parents' safety diagrams into their dreams.

"What are you doing all by yourself? How did you even get here?" Inaya's questions bounce against the walls in Deven's head. It's too late.

Deven pants, frozen in an attempt to stay out of the wasp's awareness. "What do you mean? We came here together."

"Sweety, this place is dangerous." From her signature sneakers with no laces to her shiny, jet-black hair, nearly five times longer than Deven's, Inaya is only unrecognizable by her words. Her wiggly teeth and gaps between them appear in a gleaming smile as she advances toward Deven, who treads back to protect herself from her sister. No, Inaya herself is not contagious. After all, stings themselves are what cause people to forget who they are and why they forgot. Deven just can't make this right if she gets hurt too. Her eyes race each other looking for the wasp. Or the nest. "I meant the jungle can be dangerous, not me," Inaya giggles. "But seriously, how did you get here? There's no way you were able to sneak onto my team's ship. I don't even think I ever told your mother about this survey expedition."

"You mean *our* mother? And there's no 'survey

expedition.' You were stung by one of those people-eating wasps. We have to go before the venom knocks you out. Mom and Dad might still be able to help you." Deven points a shaking arm in the direction of their family's ship.

"Ha. Ha. Very cute. Seriously though, we have to get you back to Earth on *my* ship, which is in the opposite direction."

"*Your* ship? We have one ship, and it's not that way." She drops the guiding hand to her own ship to accuse the other direction, both arms out stiff. "Now come on," she spits through gritted teeth.

"Deven is going to kill me."

"Deven? *I'm* Deven."

Inaya continues forward, condensing the space between her and Deven. "I feel like you're a little too old to be playing house. Although you do look scarily like my sister when she was younger."

"She thinks she's my aunt," Deven whispers to herself, tasting tears.

"Listen." Inaya places a hand on her relative's shoulder. "When you get to my age, you don't have time for games."

With twitching eyelids and flared nostrils, Deven slaps her sister's hand away. "Inaya!" She sucks down the heat building in her muscles, one roadkill-scented inhale after another. "I'm your twin. We're both kids. We turn ten tomorrow. That's why we're on this planet—for a family trip." That and their parents trusting that they were old enough to handle themselves.

—Ariya Bandy—

"We're going to my ship." Inaya squeezes Deven's wrists, trying to drag her in an even match of tug of war.

"Please, you have to bel—" Deven feels a pinch near her shoulder. She rotates her head, fractions of degrees at a time, to see orange and purple stripes stinger-deep in her skin. "Kiddo? What are you doing? You can't be here," she says.

***

The long-haired one collapses to the ground, greeted with thousands of wasps enveloping her skin. Watching the wasps devour their meal, the other one, still standing, doesn't move. Only her eyes enlarge on the verge of popping out. The wasps relish knowing their next meal is already in preparation, already stung.

—**Ariya Bandy** (she/her)

—Ariya Bandy—

Always

Putting the twins down is always such a chore. Olivia never wants to sleep and Violet screeches whenever Rebecca sets her abed, emerald eyes welling. Always squirming. Always screaming.

Hipping Vi, she pins Olivia down, tucks her tight. She wriggles against the sheet. Always wriggling. First kid tucked; second kid hipped. Third kid, sitting in the corner. Frosty blue eyes locked on Bec's.

No. Liv is out. Vi nearly snoring on her perch. Corner is empty.

Bec braces for wailing, lays Violet down, tucks her. Both kids are silent, and the corner is empty.

Liv's crib is empty, and little naked feet slap down the hallway. Cursing inside, Bec makes for the door, jaw already sore from clenching. A whisp of brown hair vanishes around the corner; Bec pads after.

Olivia's taking her typical route: chair, table, counter, cupboards. Exhausted arms gather the girl, shush a finger to her lips.

Back through kitchen, hallway, door to the furthest crib, where icy eyes stare up at her. Liv's in her crib but in Bec's arms. Liv's not in Bec's arms. That's not Liv in her crib. A surprised yelp; Liv drops, and Vi wakes screaming.

Both cribs are empty, both kids wailing on the floor. Bec screams too, claws her own hair. Wishes for a moment of peace, a moment alone. Without.

—Nayt Rundquist—

She breathes. Scoops a girl into each arm, moves to the reading chair across the room. Bec sits, Violet in her left arm. Liv in her right. Third child stretches a pale arm to the crib top. A second grabs hold. Third and fourth. Fifth, sixth, and more and more and more. Far-too-many arms hoist the babe up and over, drop it nimbly to the floor.

And it moves at her, all those arms crawling. Frosty eyes watching her; she watches back, glued to the chair.

Bec doesn't feel the first hand grip her ankle, or the second on her calf. But each one crawling millipede-like up her body makes her skin try to peel itself off and slough into the corner.

It burrows between the other twins; they all drift off together.

Sunlight shifts into Bec's eyes. She hoists up slow and easy, moves toward the crib. For ease, she lays them down together, backs away breathless. They're never this calm. Always squirming. Always screaming. Always watching. Putting the triplets down is always such a chore.

—**Nayt Rundquist** (they/them)

—Nayt Rundquist—

A Love Long Lost

No one remembered when the cinema had last been opened, but if you walked by in the early hours of the mornings, you would swear that it was alive. It was a beautiful building, that was certain; decked in gold and bronze and filled with the spirit of Art Deco. If you peered through the ornate glass doors, you would see the lavish imperial staircase, and the building expanding further and further backwards, full of places to explore. The lights inside always seemed to be lit, warming and dimmed. It was just so inviting. It just seemed… alive. The posters outside had long faded to nothing, but the building always seemed like it would be open to people like you.

Though it was an unlucky building as well. People spoke in hushed tones of the 1950s usherette who had fallen down the stairs and broke open her head, of the 1930s projectionist who had hung himself with the film tape, the customer from the 2000s who had had a heart attack and had just died in his seat. And those were just the people they knew about. You knew what big companies were like—and this wondrous place had been owned by so many big companies before. You knew it was likely multiple deaths had happened here and been covered up, but did it really matter? In this country, nearly every building had had one death, at the very least. It was part of being such an old country, with such old buildings. Why should this cinema be any different?

And you so wanted to visit, to go inside and marvel at the cinema in all its antique beauty. The sign hastily posted on the doors had read 'closed' for so long, but you can smell popcorn and hear laughter from inside, and the lights are on!

—*Sarah R. New*—

You feel irritation bubble in your chest as you peer again through the dusty, clouded window pane. Yes, you are right! You can see them—shadowy shapes moving in the foyer—but you pull at the door handle only for it to resist. It's locked. Desperately, you look up again and the shapes have stopped moving, the laughs have stopped, it is still. But that doesn't matter. You need to go inside.

Thinking of a strategy, you realise that you won't be able to get through the front door. They know you are there, they are guarding it. But they probably think you have given up attempting to enter, and they probably haven't expected you to slink to the old, rusted fire exit door behind the building. They probably wouldn't even think that you would be strong enough to force the door open (even you didn't), and even though it sticks, the metal has warped enough for you to contort your way inside. The lights, the sounds, the smells, you just want to be part of it all.

You slip through the cinema softly, trying not to draw attention to yourself. Trying to keep the shock off of your face, you can't believe what you're seeing. The cinema had been filled with people moving, and the sounds of voices, yes, but these beings aren't exactly what you would term people. These people are out of many times, their clothes from all sorts of periods and their skin somewhat translucent. This is why the cinema is closed off and locked up. It is not of this time. This cinema is not for the living; it belongs to the dead. A bartender stands behind the well-stocked bar—his skin jaundiced, eyes bloodshot. He winks at you unnervingly as you walk into the foyer, as if he knows that you are different to them. You hope the rest of them do not realise that one of the living is walking amongst them. You worry they won't be as accepting as the

—Sarah R. New—

bartender seems to be, although as you look back at him, his eyes still firmly locked on you, you think that his smile is not accepting but instead one of a wild animal that has locked sight on its prey. You shiver involuntarily, moving on.

An old man with a comically large walking stick sits next to an elegant lady in 1940s dress. Her neck is bent at a strangely unnatural angle, and you try not to stare at her. You walk past a young customer service assistant, probably from the 2000s if you had to guess, still wearing his work uniform. He routinely asks for your ticket, although he doesn't really look at you. You mutter something about dropping it and he just waves you through, not really caring. As you pass him, you get a better look at him, noting his singed t-shirt and hair, the smell of smoke coming off of him. He blows his nose, and you see the tissue fill with soot. You figure that all of these people died here, in one way or another. The lobby is filled with people. There are so many more than you would have expected.

You make your way to the nearest screen, just trying to get away. While initially you had been excited to visit the cinema of dreams, now you are scared, worried you'll be trapped here, your dream turning into a nightmare. But as you enter, just for a second, your fears dissipate. The red, velvet curtains; the plush vintage seats; the delicate wall sconces—this is the cinema screen you'd always imagined in your mind. You gasp, before noticing there are already two people in here. You duck, hoping that they haven't heard you, haven't seen you. But as you look on, you realise that you haven't even grazed their periphery. The young couple sit in the back, their fingers intertwined with one another's, as they gaze lovingly into each other's eyes. Young love, you think to yourself, a pang in your chest. As you look closer, you notice her pressed uniform, bow tie, open wound on

—Sarah R. New—

her temple, and the film clippings falling out of his pocket, the red ring around his neck. You know who these two are—you shouldn't interrupt them.

You make your way back to the foyer, the closest way out. Even though you've spent hours at these windows, hoping to make it inside, all you want now is to run away as far as you can. You don't belong here, you now know that, and fear being stuck here. You just about make it to the door, your arm straining to reach, when a hand clamps down on your wrist. Panic floods though you as you slowly look up into the face of the bartender, smirking at you. Casually, he takes his hand off of your wrist and pulls the door handle open, as if it had never been locked.

"You stay safe out there," he drawls, a knowing glint in his eye as you nod and step outside, watching the ghosts of the cinema fade away.

—**Sarah R. New** (she/her)

—Sarah R. New—

Untitled Crochet Works
—**Cromika** (she/her)

—Cromika—

The Four Stages of Demonic Possession

Infestation: Your sock underneath my bed, a strand of your hair on my shoulder, dried tissues. I call these love's collateral. I stopped wearing orange, started reading more on this magic pheromone perfume, and manifestation; writing your name seven times over and stuffing it underneath my mattress. I wish I looked more like a woman and not an eager schoolgirl.

Oppression: Waking dreams of your phantom touch. I can feel this rot creeping in from my ribs; it is not but an underling. I am as frail as a moth's wings.

Obsession: The taste of goblin fruit, the sweetness of sacrilege. I see you in my sleep. I see you in the shapes of leaves. The chipping oak door is the same color as your eyes. I cut my hair, frightened you'd love me less.

Possession: *Et tu, Brute?* It is a searing cruelty that bites at bone. *Do what you came for, friend.*

—Areeba Zanub (she/her)

—Areeba Zanub—

All Fairy Tales Are Horror Stories

The fairy-tale heroines chopped off their
hands to save their fathers, their fingers to
save their brothers, their tower-long hair to save
themselves. Compared to such extremes, what
I did was not insanity, not even worthy of
mention, not much at all:

I simply excavated my imperfections, gouged
them right out of my skin. Goodbye to every
bump and blemish; hello to pits and pockmarks,
swollen surfaces I could do nothing to calm,
horror I was helpless to stop.

I was trapped in the Bluebeard's castle of my
body—I had used the wrong key, peered into the
wrong room. Discovered stains I could not
scrub off.

I began to believe the only solution would be
to gouge out my eyes, stop seeing the flaws. Throw
myself from the tower in which I'd locked myself, land
on a bed of thorns, impale body and soul.

I had imagined myself Rapunzel, but instead I
became her prince—the one who had not saved
her from the witch. The one who lost his sight and
roamed desolate lands, searching for his lover or
for himself.

—Stephanie Parent—

How many tears would it take to clear my vision?
How long could I squeeze salt water from a stone?
If I walked forever, could I be rescued, could I
rescue myself, could I leave behind

the body I'd

broken?

—**Stephanie Parent** (she/her)

The Dinner Menu

I *finally* found a meat the kids would eat. The pediatrician says growing children need protein. And good mothers make sure their children get everything they need to stay happy and healthy.

Parenting books only cover the basics. These self-proclaimed "experts" don't provide any insight on how to keep *your* sanity when your children suddenly decide they hate *everything* you make. As if just trying to feed them anything remotely nutritious is a heinous crime against the very fibers of their being. The so-called experts say to keep offering the foods to your children, but how much food can I afford to waste on futile offerings?

Every meal had become a battle with loud shouts and whines of protest. Then, there was crying about being hungry because they hadn't eaten. And on top of that, my husband felt the couple of hours he was home to endure this form of torture was unbearable. He'd sit through one mealtime war, and he had had enough.

Well, *what about me?*

He was at work all day, so he deserved to have some peace, quiet, and time to relax.

Well, what about me?

Is what I do all day *not* considered work, too?

Of course, it is, he told me. He couldn't possibly do all the things that I do at home with our kids nearly as efficiently. And somebody has got to do it. I'm just "better" at it than him.

—Tinamarie Cox—

Every night, it was the same argument. He invalidated all my efforts and struggles by writing himself out of the equation. And many of the other moms in the kids' playgroup related. Except for Tanya. Apparently, she lucked out with the *best husband ever*. They're a "team." That's how you're "supposed" to do parenting.

At least I'm not the only one who rolls her eyes at Tanya's perfect life with her stain-free clothes and layers of immaculate makeup. Not that she has baggy, dark under-eye circles to cover up anyway with her "angels." She shows up to the group with organic fruits and vegetables cut into precious little shapes—because she has so much free time and her kids aren't picky eaters. She says she sleeps better knowing her children are getting their best start in life by eating healthy and being showered with all the latest parenting trends.

Fucking Tanya.

But now, I've finally found a meat my children will eat. Something sliced neatly into a lean cutlet. Something juicy roasted as a loin. Something breaded and baked. Something tossed in a skillet with the same colorful vegetables Tanya's kids eat.

The relief I feel with this has created a long-lasting euphoria. It's been a whole week without eating issues. My children eat their vegetables and get their protein like the pediatrician wants them to. They are eating balanced meals just like Tanya's kids.

And part of me wishes I could share this happy news with someone. Share this new joy with my husband.

—Tinamarie Cox—

The children have asked where their father has gone. When will he be back home? I tell them that he's closer than they know.

We're all closer now than ever.

I'm not looking forward to the day I have to say goodbye to him completely.

—**Tinamarie Cox** (she/her)

Elf

—After Gilbert K. Chesterton's 'The Song of Elf'

Blue-eyed   Elf
   womanish
yet heavy   hand
      upon the
      stirred   strings of
      but four or five,
   heart of each man   in him
like a babe buried   .
   they felt the   folk-s
spread
      heard the go d

            of the folk-songs,
      the gifts   o the tree,
where the girls give ale
and   tears come   .
The mighty   womanlike
      pleasure in their pain;
as he sang,

                  in vain.
As he sang   beautiful,

till the world was like a sea of tears
         a wave.

—Jack Dunlop (they/them)

—Jack Dunlop—

Corpse Melody

Sometimes, the song plays on without you
and so does the dead girl at the forest's edge.
Both can fade with neglect like sun-burned mist.

Both dangle in air—unkept promises or skydivers
in slow-motion collisions. Both beg for your ear,
coax minutes from your life like a revolving Earth

should you listen. Both find a way inside your brain
(parasitic worms), hitchhiking with thumbs pressed
against your hippocampus all the way back home.

—Jennifer Ruth Jackson (she/her)

—Jennifer Ruth Jackson—

Don't ask me
—Irina Tall Novikova (she/her)

Ink, gouache on paper – Size: 10 x15 cm – 2023

—Irina Tall Novikova—

Deliver Edith

CW: blood, religious homophobia

The blood rain started early that morning. By the time Edith had sat down in front of her fire for tea and toast, everywhere was darkened by the red sky. The streets were slick with a murderous hue. Edith's pink roses in her garden were stained and tainted. She bit down and felt the greasy crumbs over her lips. She chewed slowly whilst watching the flames dance around each other, feeling their warmth radiate on her bare feet. The blood rain was heavy and she could hear it beating against her windows. She turned and looked outside, clasping her warm mug of tea. Fat, scarlet drops hammered against the glass, coating it in a gruesome glaze.

The violent flap of the letterbox startled Edith. It was a Sunday, there shouldn't be any post. She lifted herself from the sofa and walked to her door. Opening it ever so slightly, she peeked around and caught the quick movements of a figure running away. Edith frowned—she recognised the slight limp and a foul-coloured waterproof (the blood stains were an improvement). A red-spattered letter lay on her welcome mat. There were heavier stains where the sender's fingers had clamped down onto the envelope, soaked through to the letter itself when she opened it.

This is all your fault. We are paying for your sin.

Edith rolled her eyes and ripped up the letter before throwing it into the fire. The edges of the paper blackened and withered to ash as the flames took hold. The church group could not leave this earth without having the last word. Behind the mossy, stone walls of that quaint, little village church was a

—A.J. Cossey—

simmering cauldron of ignorance; the group members congregating like witches at midnight. The open arms and charitable doings faded fast when Edith's long-held secret was outed to everyone.

It started with being ignored when they gave the biscuits out, then hairs in her tea. She stuck with it but noticed that people were slowly edging their seats away from her when meetings began. She remembered that final morning, not long before the skies turned red. The Vicar met Edith outside the main doors and gave an entry price—to repent her *evil ways*. Walking away sealed her damnation. It didn't take long for word to get around the village. Soon enough, mothers were dragging children across the street to avoid her, and she was cleaning splattered eggs from her front door every week.

Edith picked up her mug and sipped her tea, now lukewarm. She almost choked when she heard the loud bang. She stood and waited—another bang. Following the sound, she crept towards the dining room and looked to the bay window at the front of the house. There, flattened against the glass were two dead crows. They slid downwards, their wings twitching. Edith went to move closer but staggered backward again as another crow hit the window. Then, a wood pigeon followed. The birds were falling, weighed down, and consumed by the blood rain. Edith went back to her door and rattled the locks a few times to check they were in place.

Another bang. Edith went back to the window—a dove was flattened to the glass. Edith's brow furrowed as she inspected them. They looked like the church doves, the ones Karen, the Vicar's wife, kept in a custom coop in the gardens. She screamed when another dove splattered against the

—A.J. Cossey—

window, its beak wide open in a silent scream and its neck twisted to the side. She looked out onto the street and saw another figure, tall and thin, also in a waterproof coat but this time it was pink under the red haze. They had their hood up and their face was obscured like the first figure. The one with the limp grabbed something from the ground. When they stood, they held a white, feathered clump in their hand. They reared back and launched another dove at the house.

Edith drew the curtains and there was a sickly smack. She backed away, ran upstairs to her bedroom, and slammed the door shut. Standing there, Edith waited, but there was only the sound of the blood raining outside. She sunk onto her bed and breathed deeply. Gripping the quilt, she ran the comfortable softness against her hands. Edith's mind was beginning to drift, to her—to Diane. There was always a chance that her confession could push Diane away, but she had gone sixty years with a secret burning inside of her. They had been friends for so long, and she watched as Diane was pursued by men, rash and salivating like hungry wolves. Edith wanted to feel the softness of kissing Diane's cheek, the tenderness of holding her hand. She would have bought Diane flowers and spent her life making sure Diane knew she was loved. On the day that Diane had announced her engagement to a sharp-jawed man with the biggest house in the village, Edith felt like a lead weight had been dropped deep into her gut. Though she was being sucked into a vacuum of sadness, she smiled and wished Diane happiness. However, there was a charge between them, something electric that made them feel alive and giddy. To the outside world, they were just the very best of friends, but they were scared, and both of them hid in different ways. At night, Edith wondered if Diane snored or talked in her sleep, what her

—A.J. Cossey—

dreams were, and how she would protect Diane from any nightmares.

Maybe it was because time was passing her by, but Edith was finding it harder each day to bury who she was and her feelings for Diane. The husband had been gone for some time, but Edith was a cliff that was slowly being battered by waves over the years. A piece had finally broken free and fallen into the water, causing ripples and distorting the surface. So, Edith wrote the note and stashed it away in her handbag with the hope of finding Diane after the church meeting. But it fell out and landed in the unholy paws of the Vicar before she could save herself. Diane hadn't attended church since then. Now, as the blood rain poured and the birds fell from the sky and the world choked, Edith just wanted to hold Diane close as they faced the end together.

There was a crash behind Edith and she launched herself away from her bed. Shards of glass littered the floor, and ruby droplets flecked through from the hole in the window. Edith searched the carpet and saw a stone with a bloody handprint pressed into its crevices. She looked up and out of the window and down towards the street below. There were more of them now, grouped in a threatening formation—the one who had posted the letter stood at the front. They held a large, wooden cross in front of them, with what looked like a doll nailed onto it. Edith looked closer and gasped, as she realised it was a puppet of her. A large, rusty nail pierced through the puppet's heart, holding it to the wood. Its eyes were scratched out and it was stained with red as the rain kept falling. Birds kept falling from the sky, plummeting into trees and houses. The cross bearer then reared their arms up high towards the

—A.J. Cossey—

scarlet sky and slammed the cross down into the flower beds before they issued a final warning:

"Deliver yourself to us, Edith, deliver yourself unto Him! Make this right! We should not die because your sins have angered Him! This was not the great flood that was foretold! We will not be saved unless He is appeased by your death!"

Edith froze. She knew that voice—the Vicar had led the church group to her door. She flew down the stairs, her bare feet slamming down into each step as she went. As she reached the dining room, there was another crash. Edith turned back towards the stairs and pressed herself against the wall, holding her hand tightly to her mouth. There was a crunch as boots met glass in the room next to her. As they moved away, Edith slowly edged into the kitchen. She kept low so as not to attract the attention of those still waiting outside. The blood rain roared and they were now chanting:

Cleanse the world of sin, deliver Edith unto Him.

Another stone and more glass lay next to what used to be her bay window. What was worse, there were bloody bootprints that led from the broken window into the house. Panic rose in Edith's chest and a sickly hot drop fell in her stomach. She inched her hands towards her pruning shears that were on the kitchen table, grabbing them tight and holding the handle just in front of her chest. She kept her back towards the counters, dodging behind the small island in the middle of the kitchen. She stopped as she heard the heavy footfalls start again. Glass broke under their tread as they stalked past the kitchen, and Edith took her moment when she heard them reach the stairs. She darted out of the kitchen and made her way to the

—*A.J. Cossey*—

living room where she saw her salvation—her French doors that led to the back garden.

Cleanse the world of sin, deliver Edith unto Him.

Suddenly, a great force fell upon Edith's shoulders and threw her backward. The air was knocked out of her as she landed on her back and the pruning shears fell away from her as the Vicar held her down by her neck. He snarled and spittle fell upon Edith's cheeks.

"YOU WILL REPENT!" he screamed.

Edith's hands rose and clawed at his face as his hands clamped hard around her throat. The world began to blur, her temples were throbbing but she felt the soft, rubbery eyelids on the Vicar's face, before gouging into his eyes with her thumbs. He tried to wriggle his head away but refused to let go of Edith, and her hands had a tight grip. The Vicar's eyes popped like crushed grapes. He fell backwards screaming. Edith coughed and wheezed as she gulped air into her lungs.

Cleanse the world of sin, deliver Edith unto Him.

The Vicar flailed on the floor, clasping his now empty eye sockets and hurling damnations at Edith. She got back on her feet, picked up the pruning shears from the floor, and headed towards her exit again, but a scream interrupted her. Edith turned around. Another one of the group, the one wearing the pink waterproof, had also entered through the smashed window upon hearing the Vicar's cries of pain. They froze at the blinded man flopping like a fish out of water. They launched after Edith, who, without thinking, sunk the pruning shears into their throat.

—A.J. Cossey—

All was still. The blood rain hammered outside and the attacker's hood fell away. Edith hovered as the blades of the shears were embedded in Karen's throat. Edith stared at Karen's face, blank, wide-eyed, and twitching as she struggled to breathe. Edith yanked out the shears and Karen's blood sprayed out before the drained body collapsed on the floor.

Cleanse the world of sin, deliver Edith unto Him.

Edith stood still, gripping the shears. She wiped Karen's blood from her eyes and looked down—her pale, wool jumper was drenched, the little embroidered daisies coated in the red spray.

"If your God is righteous, I don't think you'll be meeting Him," muttered Edith.

She looked around at her decimated house. Karen's body lay still. The Vicar's cries now became whimpers as he crawled around on his belly to try and find a way out. Edith was satisfied that he would meet the end terrified and in total darkness.

Cleanse the world of sin, deliver Edith unto Him.

She inhaled sharply and looked towards the front door. Defiance thrummed in her heart. Death was coming for everyone, but she would not let it find her in her tainted home. Edith walked to her front door and slid the locks open. Her hand hovered over the handle for a moment before she stepped outside.

A sticky flood of rushed into the house behind her and pooled up to her ankles. The air outside smelled thick and metallic. The dark clouds were the colour of cabernet and swirled together angrily. Though fewer birds were falling now,

—A.J. Cossey—

the blood rain was heavier and the lightning had begun. There was a flash, Edith counted and reached five before thunder rumbled.

"It's not far away, I better get to Diane," she said to herself.

Wading forward, Edith reached her garden gate and noticed that the chanting had stopped. She looked over and met the eyes of the mob that had congregated outside her home. As she opened the gate and stepped through, the mob noticed her state, the bloodied sheers in her hand, and backed away.

"Where is the Vicar?" asked one of the group.

"Fulfilling his act of penance," Edith replied.

A few horrified gasps erupted, followed by a fluttering of Hail Marys. Edith smirked, dropped the shears into the scarlet stream below her, turned away from the horde, and began walking down the street.

The flood sloshed against Edith's ankles and up her legs as she walked. Her clothes stuck to her skin as the rain soaked them through. The incline up the street made her legs ache but she kept going. The red poured down from above and mixed with the human blood on her clothes. Shocks of lightning crackled across the sky and booming thunder followed. Edith stopped suddenly when she felt something on her foot. The carcass of a pigeon bobbed up out of the death-stream and she flailed her limbs trying to get out of the way. Edith looked; as the flood continued through the street, the dead birds went with it. She quickened her pace as the sky became more violent.

—A.J. Cossey—

Edith's hair was saturated and blood droplets ran into her eyes. She wiped away what she could, recognising where she stood. Diane's house had all of the lights on, glowing red through the windows. Edith gulped. She reached the door and hesitated for a moment before knocking. She stood for what felt like an age. Maybe Diane had left to be with family, like many others in the village who were holed up in their homes or stuck on the packed roads. This was where Edith was meant to be. Her teeth chattered as the cold wetness soaked through to her bones. The door opened, revealing a weary but beautiful Diane. Edith looked up through her blood-stained eyelashes. Diane had her arms folded and kept away from the door opening. Edith thought she might be frightened of the rain, but then she spotted the rosary in Diane's hand.

"Hello Diane," said Edith.

"Hello," Diane replied.

"You look lovely."

Lightning flashed, Diane flinched and backed from the doorway a bit more, then stepped nearer again.

"I thought you would've left by now," said Diane.

"I only want to be here. There's nowhere else I can go nor want to be."

Diane stared at Edith, her knuckles white as she gripped the rosary.

"I love you, Diane," said Edith, "I always have. Even if you don't feel the same, I can't leave this world without telling you."

—A.J. Cossey—

Thunder rocked the sky and it sounded like the raindrops were hitting an ocean. Diane relaxed her arms and walked forward. Blood speckled on her greying hair and her clothes. As Diane reached Edith, she dropped the rosary into the bloodstream below her and they stood eye-to-eye. Diane ran her hands through Edith's hair and placed them on either side of Edith's face.

"I love you too," said Diane.

She drew Edith close and their lips met. Lightning flashed again. Their arms intertwined and they kissed more urgently. They remained that way, desperate to stay close, as the red sky emptied itself around them.

—**A.J. Cossey** (she/they)

—A.J. Cossey—

Blackwater, Maine

you lose cell service driving under trees

           maybe it's because the leaves block signals

but the date and time glitch

                on your dashboard

half numbers on green scrambled screens.

you find a diner in the woods,

neon glow beaconing

            at the end of an earth road,

you wonder if they get much business

this deep into then forest.

sit at the counter,

           someone sits beside you,

a man with dry rot antlers

and eyes in his hands

you'd ask him who he is

but you know names have power.

you take your coffee black

    he takes his with nine sugars

and is careful not to close his palm around the spoon.

—Leah Barron—

when you decide to ask what he is,

his lips don't move

i am what they made me.

you don't know who they are but

the townsfolk in Blackwater seem just like that.

he tells you, coffee mug to mouth,

you should leave these woods

before you forget

where you came from.

—Leah Barron (she/her)

Ingrid M. Calderón-Collins (she/her)

—*Ingrid M. Calderón-Collins*—

Feed

Silvia had never felt a more persistent sensation than the gnawing hunger that had plagued her for the past week. What had started as a desire to cook a fuller breakfast than usual one morning had steadily grown into an insatiable hunger. She had spent the day sitting in a buffet from breakfast until they were giving her judgmental side eyes well into dinner service, and even that had failed to make a dent in the yawning void.

Clutching her cramping stomach while it groaned, begging for more, she doubled over in the driver's seat of her beat-up car. She slammed a fist against the wheel, cursing.

She watched a family loading into the car beyond the couple of empty spaces beside her, their full stomachs leaving them content at best, regretfully nauseous at worst. She frowned deeply as her own rattling emptiness deepened. Jealousy of their ability to eat to that point washed over her until another intense stomach cramp ripped through her abdomen, causing her to white-knuckle the wheel.

The first appointment available at her doctor's office wasn't for another nine days.

Driving back to her small house was difficult, but sleep was proving to be impossible. She had cleaned out the pantry and refrigerator quickly, and she was already rationing her remaining savings to survive until payday. The idea that she was struggling to survive made her scoff and roll over in bed, pulling the comforter tightly around her shoulders.

An increase in appetite wasn't a death sentence—she was consuming plenty of calories a day to keep her body alive.

—Vix Martin—

Although, it seemed like the hunger was accompanied by an increased metabolic rate that had kept the pounds off so far.

A panel of light fell across her face, causing her to squint, raising a hand to shield her eyes. For a brief moment she heard a shuffle followed by a sharp, wet impact that rattled the windowpane. Silvia sat up with a grumble, pushing her messy hair from her face as she swung her feet out of bed. She stumbled on an uneven board as she padded across the frigid wood.

The curtain hooked on the bar, resisting her attempt to pull it aside until she jostled the fabric with a correctly angled upwards toss combined with a yank. White light reflected back from a coat of freshly fallen snow to wash out her room, applying a pale filter to existence as her eyes adjusted.

The stain in the center of the window was the first thing Silvia noticed. She traced the smear of the lower half to gauge the angle the bird fell to the ground, finding a Mourning Dove resting in a pile of soft powder. Fat snowflakes drifted lazily from a sky of low purple clouds that reflected the lights of town to create a facsimile of daylight. The dove's neck was twisted around, protruding at an unnatural angle. Blood had splattered across the snow as it fell.

Silvia swallowed hard, fingers spread and hands flexing in a jerking motion.

While they hadn't been too common of a staple in her house growing up, she had eaten a variety of fowl in the past. A dove wasn't too far off from, say, a quail.

Her mouth was watering as the dead bird began to steam in the snow as its body heat escaped. She rubbed her eyes, making the

—Vix Martin—

steam dissipate into the night.

An old sweatshirt for a college she hadn't gone to hung on the back of her door. She threw it on in a desperate rush as she stomped into a pair of wool lined boots, throwing open the bedroom door and hurrying through her house. She didn't realize she was running until she had to come to a complete stop to force the back door open. Fumbling with the doorknob, Silvia was growing increasingly frustrated; the feeling in her stomach was echoing out through her torso, vibrating her ribs, increasing pressure on all of her organs, increasing her frenzied heartbeat until it buzzed in her ears. Tension built up across her forehead, pressure filling her sinuses until she felt like she couldn't breathe.

The door finally gave way to her clumsy attempts, the knob twisting with her clammy palm and swinging open.

Stillness stretched through the night, amplifying each time it came into contact with either the dense clouds or the soft carpet of snow, until the silence became a deafening noise unto itself.

Silvia didn't let the oppressing sensation stop her, sliding awkwardly as she made her way down the icy stairs into the yard. The second to last step took her balance out from under her, sending her swiftly to the ground. Her hands and knees crushed into the snow. She couldn't stop moving, just the exertion of getting to the door had been enough to send the hunger pangs into her chest.

It didn't matter to Silvia that her pajama pants were soaking wet or that her hands were on fire as she crawled to the bird. There wasn't a moment of hesitation as she took hold of the still-warm corpse and tore off a section of bloody breast meat and feathers

—Vix Martin—

with her teeth. Her hands had torn the bird in half.

"Oh, fuck yes," she sighed, chewing contentedly as she slumped against the wall, shirt catching on the rough brick. Through her closed eyes, the dove was delectable, soaked in a divine rum sauce, and decorated with a light dusting of breadcrumbs. She had never eaten something so tantalizingly delicious.

Another bite, the head taken all at once and swallowed with a pleasured moan.

Nothing she had gorged herself on the past few days had been quite so intriguing, so enjoyable. So satisfying.

Silvia actually experienced a moment of relief as she sat in soaked fleece. What a tease a moment can be.

The hunger returned quickly, a renewed depth stretching inside her. Silvia pushed her head against the wall with a sharp exhale, shoving her hands into her tangled hair to press hard on either side of her skull. She swore through her teeth, grinding them together to match her squeezing. Her fingers adhered to loose strands as they pulled away, the tug pulling her vision back into focus. Blood and small feathers coated her hands.

Before the shock could form into a full thought, the pain crescendoed to a new peak, forcing her to double over.

MORE.

The only thought that could form in her mind.

MORE. MORE.

—Vix Martin—

Her eyes snapped back and forth, scanning her surroundings for anything, any movement, any signs of life only to find nothing but the blurring white lines of the lawn furniture.

There wasn't anything *more*, at least, not here.

But the longer she sat in the deepening feeling of hunger, the less restrained she realized herself to be; not here, but maybe elsewhere.

Silvia stood on a lawn chair to stare into the large back window of the house next to hers. They didn't have a motion light like she did, so it wouldn't take much to get up to their back door.

Hopping the fence, the powder silencing her impact, she crept to the porch steps. An unlocked, rubber-flap pet door caught her attention, just big enough for her to shimmy inside. Even if the pressure ripped her clothing and scratched her arms, it wouldn't matter.

A dog was quick to greet her with a low growl followed by an immediate, sharp bark.

Silvia shushed it, holding up both hands to pull herself forward across the tile while clinging low to the ground.

"Hey boy," she said soothingly, if higher pitched than her normal tone. "Hush now—shut up!"

The closer she came, the more defensive the animal got, letting off another small set of warning barks. A shout came from the far end of the house.

"Dumb ass dog, go back to bed! It's nothing!"

—Vix Martin—

An obviously exhausted statement that made it clear that midnight barking was a common bad habit. Silvia wagged her finger at the dog, which continued to growl as she crept closer, sunken low on her hips. She approached the dog, reaching out an inquisitive hand that was met with a defensive snap.

"You really are a dumb ass dog," she sneered, hand snapping out to wrap around the animal's throat. No more potentially alarming noises could be made after she strangled the dog in its bed.

The kitchen was well stocked, she could tell even in the dark. Her eyes had dilated so that she could make out the twilight-grey details. Shelves and counters loaded down with food sat high above where she was crouched, but Silvia couldn't bring herself to stand. Not when she kept getting distracted by the fresh meat immediately beside her. The dog radiated warmth, much more than the bird had, and she salivated to think of what it might taste like.

The first bite was taken from the shoulder, which was tough to tear away. The mouthful had an explosively exquisite flavor. Silvia threw her head back in delight as blood coated her chin.

Despite the effort required to break the skin, the flesh was tender as if it had been slow roasted over an open fire. The fur formed a char more flavorful than any she had ever tasted before.

Bringing her mouth to the carcass, she tore away another hunk of meat while savoring the unique, gamey flavor. One bite blended into the next until she was tearing away chunks, repeatedly swallowing them whole.

Skin across her abdomen pulled taut over a distending stomach.

—*Vix Martin*—

Silvia groaned in satisfaction as she felt relief yet again fluttering in her mind, intangible and impossible to pin down. The light flickered brightly as she ate, but began to dim with the warmth of the food. Each bite became less satisfying until Silvia was sobbing as she chewed and forced down another hard swallow.

MORE

"Why isn't this enough?" she hissed, slamming the heels of her hands into her head.

*MORE MORE MORE **MORE***

A noise, down the hallway opposite where the annoyed voice had originated. A door creaked open to slowly spill a pale yellow light on a short hallway. The kitchen island stood between her and them, giving Silvia a moment to slip beneath the blanket in the dog's bed, forcing the rigid corpse back to tangle with the fabric as she pulled it over herself.

"Barnaby?" a small voice whispered as the sound of quiet footsteps padded onto the kitchen tile. "You okay, boy?"

The slurred late-night whisper of a child attempting to keep from being caught while doing something they shouldn't.

The throbbing desire shifted from a solid thought to a wordless, constant urge driving her forward. It merged with her heartbeat,

—Vix Martin—

deafening her with doubling fervor each pulse deep in her ears.

MORE

Silvia laid still in the dark, obscured by the blanket as the child crept closer.

Her mouth was dripping with saliva, stomach growling with the constant, horrible hunger.

She could just barely make out the silhouette of the child as they leaned down towards the dog bed.

MORE

The child lifted the blanket, squinting for its dog in the darkness. "Barnaby?"

Silvia's hands shot out, grabbing tight to the child's shoulders to pull it down. Her jaw stretched open as she sank her teeth into the soft skull, mouth straining around it, the skin where her lips met straining as the child kicked and screamed. There was a grotesque ripping sound as her own blood mixed with the viscera while her jaw expanded enough to begin the act of swallowing them whole.

Ambrosia.

The voice demanding *more* was silenced as her eyes rolled back in her head while devouring a whole, living being. The flavor

—*Vix Martin*—

was indescribable, perfect.

The child slid down her throat twitching as its parent ran screaming down the hallway, pumping a shotgun.

Silvia knew true bliss in the moments before her brains were splattered across the floral kitchen wallpaper.

—**Vix Martin** (they/them/fae/faer)

—Vix Martin—

Pillars of Salt
—**Carella Keil** (she/her)

—*Carella Keil*—

"and that these actions did not at any time constitute a criminal act"

I don't think
you need to worry.
I don't think you should
worry over me.
He would never touch me.
He never did put his big hands
on my breasts.
He didn't pull my hips against him
although he may have let his fingers wander
over my chilly bare feet.
He just wanted to have a look.
He just thinks he can make suggestions
for my body's marketability,
suggest renovations or repairs,
a darker shade of nail polish,
Jergen's cream or a half-hour
lifting sore arms to twist the curling iron.
I mean, I have an ass
and he has eyes.
He isn't blind, you know,
and when I was dieting and crying,
I looked almost like my mother.

Anyway, I'm safe now.
I'm not his type anymore.
I gained weight when I moved out of his house
and stopped starving myself.

—Sophie Farthing—

He'll never see Mom's head
on my shoulders again
since I shaved off all my hair.

—**Sophie Farthing** (she/her)

A.B.B.Y

Marina had been sitting out in her car, enveloped by the afternoon, for the better part of an hour. The deeply tinted lip balm she had smeared on her cracked lips had smudged, and, after fixing it, she finally ran out of things to do.

***

The Institute shone, an obnoxious phallus at the end of the car park. She approximated it would take her 2 and a half minutes to walk the length of the parking lot and arrive at the colossal magnetised gates. She approximated this because it always did take her exactly 2 and a half minutes. Marina had, over the years, learned that this was the exact amount of time she could hold her breath. She never breathed the length of it, appearing at its great mechanic gates dizzy and world-fuzzed. Today, she worried she would be particularly slow to cross the liquifying asphalt. Looping her security pass around her neck, she swung out of the car and into the cakey day's air. Before her mind could catch up, her legs had made swift and regular movements, and the security booth stood inches before her. As if on cue, the guard cleared his throat, "Are you feeling any better today Ms. Menkin?"

She flushed. The already dampening patches at the bottom of her spine and armpits seemed to widen and cling impetuously to her shirt. She was annoyed that they kept the same day staff on so frequently, this one was here the last time, and evidently remembered.

"I am, as a matter of fact, Frank." She had not intended to sound curt, but the words came out as nails fire from a gun.

—Stephanie Ritzema—

"Thank you," she added, softening.

"How is Shelley?" she continued, but he had already buzzed her ID through and his response as to the general wellbeing of his wife lost itself to the fading distance of the amniotic afternoon. Entering, every detail of the place came into an uncomfortably clear view. The pale sheen of the great doors, the giant lettering that read "Carnegie Rock-Hertig Institute for Reproductive Sciences,' and the fumigating hiss of clean, cool air, became such acute experiences that Marina found herself nauseous and had to steady herself.

She waved a two-fingered gesture at the receptionist, smiling wetly.

I will remain as always she almost muttered for comfort, and self-congratulated at having pulled off the wave with a degree of normalcy. But before indulging in the brief respite of the mind, the waifish receptionist tittered

"How are you feeling today Ms. Menkin? Are you doing any better?"

After receiving no response, she added, "We were all a little worried about you—we thought you wouldn't wake up!"

With this, the receptionist laughed, a high, tinny laugh that dipped up at the end, as if she had noticed she had said something a little wrong and was now trying to suck the words back into her face.

"I am perfectly fine now, thank you, Samantha. Was just a little light-headedness, was all." Marina slipped out and took no more time clicking her way down the barren corridor, away from the prying eyes of young Samantha.

—*Stephanie Ritzema*—

A person faints once, and everybody talks about it for weeks she thought to herself. When, in reality, she herself had thought about it for weeks. Throughout her entire medical career, she had never once fainted. Not in the dissection rooms, not at the blood and bile, not even when her fellow junior doctors had inflated a sheep's lung past the point of tensile strength. While her colleagues had fled and fell like flies in winter, she had remained resolute and simply wiped the debris from her goggles with one steady hand.

***

The episode from her last visit to the Institute was unique in another way. It was, consequently, her eventual reason for visiting today. Her reason for each step she took nearer to the room.

She reached the lift and paused to take a gulping breath before stooping slightly to press the lowermost button on its reflective control panel—

Room A.B.

—it read and gleamed, like a possessed red circle against the scrubbed backdrop. The lift whizzed its usual insect hum and skittered every couple of moments. Marina prayed no one would call it, and as if granting her some barely afforded pleasure, it sank down without interruption and landed with an unheard thump into its final undercroft.

Marina was catatonic. The bile had reached her throat and was threatening to penetrate the pinched corners of her mouth. Her palms no longer palms but acrid and sogged extensions of her arms that hung limp about her chest, cupping her breasts as if to shield them.

—Stephanie Ritzema—

She was not afraid of what she saw when the lift doors opened—because what is there to be scared of in something you have seen so many times before? Perhaps it was the a discomfort at the familiarity and the knowledge that what lay at the end of that vast and expansive room was something that no human should ever feel comfortable around or familiar with. She stepped out.

The usual dull thuds and hiss of medical equipment echoed through the walls and moved like a snake about the claggy basement air. The room always smelled faintly of ammonia, and the thick rubber scent of old hospitals. It was consistently just slightly darker down here than even the dimmest rooms upstairs. Years ago, Marina had attempted to put this in with the one person aware of the room's existence in the head office. She was quickly silenced and sent to another room where she sat knocking at the doctor's door, to no saintly avail.

And there, at the end of the room, unchanging, was the tank. Glowing blue against a veil of gun grey, the thing had always appeared too large for what it was. Obviously it had to be made larger over the years so as to accommodate for its inhabitant's growing body. The bubbles in the fluid plucked themselves up and danced their way around yellowish tubes, as if performing heinous coquettish pirouettes for the rare spectator. The sign in the left-hand corner remained unchanged:

PROJECT 1:   **"A.B.B.Y"**

Marina approached, but remained at a distance, taking in the entire boundless thing at once.

—Stephanie Ritzema—

148

"Hello Abby."

The voice that returned was garbled and sounded as though someone was speaking through a tube underwater. It was always deeper than Marina was prepared for.

"Hello Mother," the word sent a fresh spike of ice through Marina's nervous system and she teetered on her heels. What had she thought, all those years ago, when the thing first learnt to speak and she had allowed it to address her as *mother?* She supposed she had let it address her that way because, in more than just a manner of speaking, it was true.

"How are you today, Abby?" Marina managed to heave out from her dry lips.

The voice came again, "I am growing again, Mother." And then, after a pause, "It hurts."

At this, Marina's head fell forward begging to erase the image of the large gelatinous thing in front of her from any crevice of her working memory. It hurt. Another noise came.

"You...are...ill....Mother?   You...are...never...ill?"   This time, as it spoke, the words dragged like feet in clay, and an emery board laugh coughed through the fizzing mouth tube.

Marina chewed the inside of her gums and fought the tears back, tooth and nail, from crashing; she would not prolong the sickening truth any longer. Suppressing a cacophonic nausea she spoke, "I am very ill." She paused, "I don't believe anyone has ever told you about cancer, have they?" Her voice plummeted, a tone of acceptance on the horizon of the vowels.

"A...man...once...told...me...I...am...a...cancer..."

—Stephanie Ritzema—

Marina was confused for a moment. She thought she should remember this. Then she realised the thing was referring to its own father.

"No. You are not a cancer."

"What...is...cancer?"

"Cancer—" She stopped, suddenly numb. She was trying to hustle the words that the unfeeling doctor had used into her brain, but she could only think of cartoon crabs, and her only son's birthday.

"Cancer means—" She stooped to rectify her heel strap, "—I am going to die." She spoke this in the tone you would use to highlight an obvious mistake.

"Soon." She added.

"I am going to die soon, and you will be alone."

The thing did not respond, but only released a low melancholic drone, that may, in another life, have been a cry.

"You...promised...me...You...said...I...would...be...more... You...said...I...would...be...free..." it wailed.

And, as if it had never once occurred to her, Marina quietly realised her cruelty in the lying. She had often told it that one day, maybe, it would roam free. That the planet would allow such an abominable hunking piece of continuously-growing, always-dividing flesh into its domain. Perhaps there would be space in our world for a foetus as wide as a temple. But she had known there never would be, and Marina had wondered what a woman was to do when her child was crying.

—Stephanie Ritzema—

"I know my love, I know, I am sorry," she glided forward and placed first one hand, then two, and then the side of her face against the cool clear glass. The final plug she intended on pulling lay only two feet from her on the left, behind a stock of tubes and wires.

"I am so sorry little one, I am so sorry."

"Don't..." It whispered. "Don't...leave...me."

She remembered Daniel, and his hatred for her. All her hours at work, all the pain she bore for him, the countless hours slaving day-in-day-out over the stove and the washer and the dryer, all to the sound of his tinny voice screaming, demanding always, wanting always, more, more, more. When she had told him she had uterine cancer he just sighed, left to make a cup of tea, and exclaimed, "finally we can put the dozy bint in a care home."

She decided she was tired. So. Very. Tired.

Before her brain allowed her to think she replied, "I won't." Her hands reached for the plug and instead found the ladder that scaled the entire length of the upright vessel and she clasped the rungs. Bending knee after knee, she reached the top and the open blue poured out in front of her like a tide. This was it. They had given her a month, but it had taken her a week. As she grabbed the tube that sustained the heart of her beloved creation, she pushed off from the ledge and into the warm lagoon of flesh. Yanking hard, she thrust the tube up and out of the thing and in the last beat of that enormous heart muttered, "Baby, my baby."

As she sank beneath the surface of that liquid life-blood, she thought of Omickle, of lavender and powerful herbs, and of

—*Stephanie Ritzema*—

Demeter, who in the final hours turned to scorching the heavens and the Earth, speaking only,

"I am for you, my child."

—**Stephanie Ritzema** (she/her)

—Stephanie Ritzema—

Hidden Face
—Irina Tall Novikova (she/her)

Ink on paper – Size: 10 x 15 cm – 2023

—Irina Tall Novikova—

Screech Owl

The bible wouldn't have me.
I saw to that.
I've been shirking Eve
From the start.
Each box smashed—
Each leash snapped—
Every growl from my lips—
All mine, hard-won.
I keep your name
Mounted above my fireplace,
Conquered.
I took your eyes
When I left, but now
They see my smile
For the first time—
Briefly—
Before that first bite.

—Blayne Waterloo (they/she)

—Blayne Waterloo—

Footsteps in the Mist

The hair on the back of the young woman's neck stood on end as she pulled the baby out of the car seat. Dusk had settled and a creeping, crawling mist was making its way up the banks of the Sacramento River. It scooted along the ground, twisting and turning between the walnut and almond trees, covering everything in its wake as it crept toward her car and the steps leading up to the front door of the rickety singlewide house trailer she'd rented for herself and her son.

The mist came in at the same time every evening, and every evening she tried to be home ahead of it. To be up in the house that was balanced on stilts against the possibility of rising river water. To be up in the house with the door firmly locked, the windows closed tight, and the curtains drawn before the mist swirled around the stilts and wormed its way up onto the high porch. Before it pushed at the door and banged against the metal siding of the flimsy home. If she turned on the lights, every light—even the one over the sink and the one on the porch and the one in the bathroom and the one in the baby's room and the one in the living room and the lamp in her makeshift bedroom that was really a covered porch—then, she could pretend. Pretend that the mist was a normal everyday, cozy fog. That the warm glow of the lights inside her home were simply because the night was dark out here in this almond orchard where no one else lived but her and her boy. Pretend that night terrors didn't howl around the corners and whip through the trees overhead.

Tonight, her boss needed her to stay. "Just a few extra minutes," he'd said, "so I can run to the bank." She rang up

—Paula Charles—

customers, handed out roast beef sandwiches and packets of sauce, all the while biting her nails to the quick. When the boss pulled into the parking lot, she tore off her apron and ran out the back door as he was coming in the front. There was no time for pleasantries when she picked up the baby from the sitters. No time for the red light in the middle of town. She gassed the engine of her teal Dodge Colt, ignoring the finger the old man in the crosswalk threw her way.

Now the mist licked at her heels as she raced up the clackety wooden stairs. A wispy thread of gray-green haze wound around her ankles and slunk through the doorway even as she slammed the metal door closed and turned the lock. She was so focused on getting all the lights turned on that she failed to notice as it seeped under the couch and disappeared from view. The baby chortled and waved his chubby arms, waiting for the mist to come back out of its hiding place to play a game of peek-a-boo.

The young woman let out a sigh of relief. Safe. They had made it. Just barely, but that was enough. Tonight would be the last night. Tomorrow she was taking her precious son and moving far away from this unearthly terror. To a place it would never find her. Never find him. She tossed her car keys on the counter and flipped on the tv, turning the old brown knob until the tinny sound of laughter from Seinfeld filled the room and pushed back her fear. She plopped the baby in his highchair, tied a bib around his roly-poly neck, and opened a jar of baby food with a satisfying pop. The baby ate, giggling and squirming as his mom fed him. All the while, the young woman was oblivious to the mist that crept out from under the couch, scooting down the dark hallway while she had her back turned. The baby laughed and cooed.

—Paula Charles—

Later that night, with the baby tucked sleeping and warm inside his crib, the young woman ran a bath. To better hear if the baby cried out, she turned off the television, grabbed a book, and sank into the silky comfort of the warm water. After reading until she couldn't keep her eyes open, she leaned back in the tub and drifted off to sleep.

Heavy footsteps came down the hallway, stopping right outside the bathroom door. Her eyes flew open. Listening. Waiting. Had she drifted off? Was it just her terrified imagination? No. The footsteps echoed again, carrying on towards the living room. She called out.

"Who's there?" Her voice sounded thin and scared, even to her own ears. "Hello?"

Water splashed, flooding the floor as she stood. She wrapped a blue threadbare towel around her slender frame and opened the door. A blast of cool air hit her warm body, making her shiver from head to toe. Looking one way down the hallway and then the other, nothing seemed out of place. She hurried to the baby's room, dripping water as she went. Quietly she peeked over the crib railing. There he was, zipped up in a green, fuzzy sleeper, pink cheeks and a smile on his small face as he slept. She touched his warm forehead and turned, heading the other direction to patrol her small home. Nothing strange in the living room either. Everything was fine in the kitchen.

"You have lost your mind," she whispered to herself.

The bathwater had turned cold, so she pulled the plug and stepped back into the tub, turning on the shower instead. She lathered up her hair, soaped her body, and shaved her legs and armpits. She set the razor on the side of the tub, readying

—Paula Charles—

to rinse her hair, as heavy footsteps sounded once again in the hallway. Just as before, the footsteps seemed to pause outside the bathroom door. She stood still as a frightened doe. Suddenly a footstep echoed, but this sound was inside the bathroom. Three steps and they—it—was at the bathtub. As she watched, silent as a tomb, too terror-stricken to make a sound, the plastic shower curtain was shoved in at her, the imprint of two large hands clearly visible against the thin curtain. The hands released the curtain, shoving again and again.

She finally found her voice, letting out a scream that reverberated off the wall, bounced under the door and filled the trailer from corner to corner. The baby woke with a startled cry. The young woman bounded out of the shower, shampoo forming her hair into a startled scream piled high on her head. The bathroom door crashed open and she flew to the crib, scooping up the baby boy and cradling him against her wet chest. She lay him on her bed, keeping one hand on his chest as she wiggled into a pair of purple sweatpants and an oversized black sweatshirt that clung to her wet skin like desperation.

The night was black, deep and long. She kept vigil, bolt upright on the couch, eyes wide and alert, legs curled under her as the baby slept on her chest. Every noise jerked her head around, ready to fight whatever evil entity had invaded her house.

With the pink light of morning dawning, outside of the trailer the mist gathered itself up and crept back to the river. If the young woman had been watching, she would have seen the shape of an enormous man form before the mist spooled and whirled, falling into the depths of the dark water. There it—

—Paula Charles—

he—would build his energy while the world bustled. When night fell, he would be back to try again.

Once the birds begin to chirp and twitter, the woman knew it was safe to emerge. The baby awoke needing a diaper change. She cleaned him up, fed him breakfast, then turned on the mobile and put him back in the crib to chortle and laugh at the spinning turtles and fish.

Back in the shower, she quickly washed and rinsed her hair. Turning off the water, she stepped out of the tub, and her eyes flew to the words written in the steam on the mirror.

YOU WILL NOT LEAVE ME

At a frantic pace, she tossed clothes, diapers, formula, and baby food in a diaper bag, then packed a duffle bag for herself with a few things she couldn't live without. With one swipe of her arm, she cleared out the medicine cabinet and threw makeup and hairspray in a plastic grocery bag. She folded up the playpen and crammed it in the trunk of her small car, strapped the baby in the car seat, and sped down the driveway. Gravel sprayed from underneath her fleeing tires and, in the rearview mirror, the door to the rented trailer hung open, inviting anyone, anything, inside.

The young woman drove as fast and as far as she could get before exhaustion had her pulling into a one-story, horseshoe-shaped motel in the desert of western Arizona.

After a night of dreamless sleep, she woke refreshed to the sound of the baby talking and cooing to himself. Stepping outside the motel door, she took a deep, cleansing breath of the dry, desert air. Across the street, the window of an all-night café

—Paula Charles—

sported a help wanted sign. She smiled. Luck was on her side today.

A quick interview secured her the job. Her new boss introduced her to an old man with a furnished casita for rent on the edge of town. She followed the man's relic of a red truck as it bounced down a dirt driveway. The casita was a square, tan stucco cottage with a cozy living room and a kitchen with colorful tile floors. A small bathroom was tucked between two light-filled bedrooms. A quick look around outside revealed a little courtyard with natural vegetation and a cedar privacy fence. She smiled. There was no river in sight. The young woman felt at home. She paid the deposit and the first week's rent, promising him the rest with her first paycheck from the café.

The sun was setting in glorious shades of purple and orange as she unloaded the last of their scant belongings from the car. She rocked the baby to sleep while the last of the sun's rays seeped away, peacefully unaware of the mist crawling out of the covered well behind the house, taking the form of a ghoulish man, before slipping back to the ground and turning to a gray-green haze to crawl under the cedar fence and towards her back door.

—**Paula Charles** (she/her)

—Paula Charles—

Lucy Westenra, Somnambulist

> *"Lucy Westenra, but yet how changed. The sweetness was
> turned to adamantine, heartless cruelty, and the purity to
> voluptuous wantonness."* —**Dracula** by Bram Stoker

"Regret explains my hesitation," I
Explained to Mina. "Three proposals. Why
Must I choose one? Two others will feel sad."
Permission granted, I'd enjoy all three—
But this exquisite fantasy is caged,
Unvoiced, restrained with all my private filths.
Somnambulist I am—as father was—
My sleepwalk self encountered entities
Whose kiss transformed plebeian stars, unleashed
A choreography of urges, strange,
Unholy, keeping night's mind delinquent,
Outcomes forbidden in my shallow past.
I owe obedience to one man now
Who taught me how to be a ghost part-time.
Like trees, we've bound ourselves below without
Burial, cocooned in soil, still sentient,
Possessed of appetites, required to feast.
Ageless, preserved, my beauty's my bait.
"Come closer, child! Let me teach you a game!
Who am I? Mistress of my darkest dreams."

—**LindaAnn LoSchiavo** (she/her)

—LindaAnn LoSchiavo—

weird sister

i howl as i think i strike a sinking moon.
the world is wilting in half,
and i can barely lift the sickle
before it hits the ground.
my back stings.
a rat runs over my shoe.
there is a corpse in place of a scarecrow,
and i don't remember how it got there
but he has my eyes.
then there is the mad girl
who spins between cornstalks.
she sings:
what are gods to men?
what are men to crows?

—**Areeba Zanub** (she/her)

—Areeba Zanub—

Untitled Crochet Works
—**Cromika** (she/her)

Closet

You go back in the closet every night. You sleep under a fabric cloud. You rest your eyes and think of the ways in which this closet is easier, the ways in which a slow suffocation is easier than a yell and a show. When you fall asleep you only dream of the ways in which this closet could hold your whole world if you had enough hangers, the velvet ones, never the plastic, you crave softness (both for yourself and others).

Outside of your closet is the world without softness, a world without your comforter, no pillows to lay on, no sheets plastered with your own future and cum. Inside of your closet is a bed and your phone, the used water bottles that never seem to make it out, your favorite socks and all of your undies. Inside of your closet is a piece of comfort you keep hidden under your pillow, in between the mattresses, like the princess and the pea. Inside your closet you are a princess and you can wear your crown, you can do whatever you want, you make the rules.

The harsh brightness of the sun never seems to leak its way into your closet. If you could hide in there forever then finally you'd be a vampire, you could lure the hot young people in just by batting your eyes, we know that it works.

But how would you afford your closet if you never leave? Vampires can't survive in a capitalist society, they are sucking the wrong thing. So you leave your closet when the day breaks through the clouds. You muster your pants and shirt into a matching set and you reset your eyes from drop dead gorgeous to just plain old beautiful, we don't need to repeat the incident

—Victoria Hood—

from last time. You moisturize and deodorize and spray your cologne that is trapped inside our noses. You put on your human suit but laying under the surface is the sucker you always are. Out in the day time you glisten when you smile, that is why you try to keep it hidden, you don't want your secret out (not everyone needs to know), you have a closet at home filled with bodies and bodies and old bodies that you've molted out of. During the day you act like this is the only body you've ever known, the only body you will ever know, during the day you act like this is your body.

But at night you lay naked with your tendons revealed, your eyes unset, uneasy, just waiting. At night you lay in your closet and wish there was a place for sex addicted vampires, that you didn't need to hide, that someone would open their veins to you and shower you in their juices. At night you think about the times when being you was okay and you hide in the corner of your closet even though you know no one is looking for you, you have the only key, you hide in your corner, scared of the dark.

—Victoria Hood (she/her)

—Victoria Hood—

After the Grimms

Footsteps lead away
in the snow, blood
filling them. Icing roof begins
to melt. Soft
dripping.

In the gingerbread hut,
fire is turning to ember.
It's quiet. The smell of
vanilla, charred flesh.
Bird heads line the window.

Urgently, cold fingers,
tapping on the door,
tapping to get inside.

There's no one
to answer. No one at all.

—**Jessica Drake-Thomas** (she/her)

—Jessica Drake-Thomas—

Wife of the Automata

Gears, wires, levers, mechanical relays, and tics, scratching, coughing, blinking, shifting of feet. There are good colors and numbers and words and textures, in superstitious abstractions of fate and luck, the same way my automata are abstractions of nervous system mathematics. One thing triggers the other. Neurons and nerve endings. Releasing impulses. Transistors to spark the motion of life in lifeless eyes and puppet limbs. The physical impulse to scratch. The inner impulse to count. I am the automata of my compulsions, the same way my creations are the compulsions of mathematics.

My wife was the only one who understood.

Sweethearts since high school, we settled down on the Mid-Atlantic coast in a quaint town with woods and trails leading out to the dunes and misty seas. I, a teacher. Her, a mortician. She had more to teach me than I had to my students. She embalmed bodies and painted makeup on their features and plugged their orifices and set them up in nice suits or dresses. She prepared coffins and set up the scenes of wakes with warm light and spanning floral arrangements. Every day she saw photos of passing faces, smiling at a flashing camera. A constant rerun. Her job as a fugue.

The crying widows and widowers and children and cousins and parents and old school chums and great friends were like actors in a theatre. All had a part. Even her. The conductor. They moved like clockwork, the same as one another. Life on the precipice of death, animating the corpse in memories. Counting bodies to get to sleep.

—Adam J. Galanski-De León—

She had a good relationship with death—something I was incredibly afraid of. It drove my greatest fears. I always had an inkling of superstition in me. Little things that triggered impulses and cycles and numerological dread. It caused me to do irrational things. Like throwing an envelope in the trash while listening to my grandfather clock tick.

1.2.3.4. 1.2.3.4.

I counted its ticking like the time signature of a song. If I didn't throw the envelope in the trash, my wife would die. So I did. And I did it on the third tick of the second measure. Three (2) is no good. When I even say three (2), I say two after under my breath to cancel out the godforsaken number. So when I landed on the third tick, I had to pull the envelope out of the garbage and try again. I tossed it in on the fourth beat, but this was of the third measure. So I pulled it out and tossed it in again on the fourth beat of the fourth measure. But that was three (2) times I had thrown it in the trash, so I had to toss it in the garbage once more. I landed it on beat two, and that was good enough for me. My wife would stay alive.

Back then it didn't happen so often. Back then I didn't let outside things control me. Though sometimes, I'd touch the color red on a blanket or a rug, or an art print, or newspaper, or wall, and that symbolized blood to me, and injury, and death, and the death of my wife, so I had to touch a cool tone, like blue or green. If I touched that red, then touched the blue, I would have to do it four times. And if that wasn't good enough, then four times more. If that was not good enough and I had to do it three (2) times, then I would also have to do it a fourth. There would be instances when I was touching back and forth red and blue four repetitions of four-time cycles to ease my nerves and

—Adam J. Galanski-De León—

reassure myself of the good luck I had restored. It was equal parts celestial and mechanical.

Honestly for a time, I felt like I had tapped into something incorporeal. Some abstract mathematical system that God used to control the world. I felt like I had figured out a puzzle. And I became a slave to it.

Things weren't always so overwhelming. For a long time, my wife and I truly enjoyed life. We travelled, and ate and drank, and indulged in performances of the arts. We collected paintings and records, film and photographs, and typewriters, and taxidermy, and books, books, books, books. My wife believed herself to be a witch. Soon enough I believed her too. She had shelves of herbs and crystals and liquids and candles, incense, and jars of who-knows-what, and occult books I dared not look into out of anxiousness.

"I am confident that life goes on," she once told me, "The universe is math. The reproduction of cells upon cells in infinite spans the same way that space stretches on and on replicating the boundaries of emptiness. It is like the big bang turned a gear and that turned another, and in no time, like fire to hay, and moths to flame, life spread and collapsed as dominoes, and bodies were born above the soil, then buried beneath it, just to grow into plants and rise again towards the sky. When I am gone, I will not be gone. No—I will be very near."

She lit a candle and set intentions. I nodded and sighed and buried my face into my book.

I was afraid of my wife. But I loved her more than life itself.

—Adam J. Galanski-De León—

It was when we traveled to Salzburg, that I became fascinated with automata. In the Gardens of Hellbrunn where we explored grottos of trick fountains and eerie scenery, Greek Gods, flickering lights, replications of ruins, mechanical calls of birds, waterwheels and lead pipes pushed through with hot air. I became intrigued with the principles and components of clockwork mechanics and animation.

Upon returning home, I began collecting. I spent my inheritance on it. Music boxes. Trebly chimes with dancing dolls. Rochat birds that chirped like sparrows. A Navy sailor which laughed like a lunatic and shook its head and swayed its arms. A bipedal brown bear wired with triggers to animate its limbs to beat a marching drum. Monkeys which boxed. Monkeys which danced. Monkeys which clapped cymbals together. Monkeys that hung by their tails on a bar and spun around in defiance of gravity. A waiter which closed a lid on gambling dice, and opened it again to reveal their moved position. Pirates motioning a pint of ale to their hairy lips. Parakeets singing in a wire bell shaped cage. French musicians strumming lutes. Women from eastern nations gently swaying, Puppies running. Jacquemarts striking bells. Tableau Mecanique of circus acts and blacksmith's forges and ships sinking on stormy seas, and nutcracker ballets. A woman playing a sad violin. I even found penny slot machines of fortune tellers and gypsies, taking questions, and giving answers, heads and hands jostling, eyes glowing red.

The parlor room of my house was filled with them. And soon I spent all my time down there, while my wife conjured spells and manifested desires, and embalmed bodies, perfected somber bouquets. We lived separate lives. Hers, the natural

—Adam J. Galanski-De León—

cycle of life and death. Mine, the cycle of gears and triggers, and numbers, and compulsions.

We weren't so different, her and I.

I was still fearful of her death.

The more automata I collected and refurbished, the more my superstitions and tics grew to unfathomable proportions. The plethora of clocks ticked on the wall, cuckoo birds calling on the hour, chimes playing, bells ringing, robins singing.

I would be tinkering with my machines, and numbers consumed my brain, causing me to sit up out of my seat, and sit back down, and if it didn't feel right, do it again, then again and again. Then I would get so anxious I would scratch my forehead, cheek, neck, and chest. In that order. And then again and again in four cycles and repetitions of four cycles. And soon I was standing up and scratching and sitting down and scratching, then coughing in sets of four on the correct metronomic rhythm of my clocks, to the point where my brain was so overloaded with superstitions and triggers and senses and fear—oh, mostly fear—that it got to the point where I forgot the fear I had in me was the death of my wife, and the fear transformed into the fear of my compulsions themselves. And that was when I lost my sentience.

My wife did die.

I was not there for her funeral. I was busy counting and touching and scratching and blinking and coughing and standing and sitting. Finding the perfect cycles and becoming the very automations that I worked on. So busy that I did not smell the sage, incense, and burning herbs, nor the stench of rot

—Adam J. Galanski-De León—

and the bile and liquid excrement I disgorged around me. And by the time I realized what it was, it was too late. I moved in rhythm with the other machines.

The drumming bears. The jacks striking bells. The dancing women from the east. The laughing clowns, and punching monkeys. My movements were mechanical. My body, gears. My actions, impulses. My bodily functions retired. I knew that she had cursed me.

So I was relieved of my fear of her death and soon had no fear at all. But my body was clockwork and cyclical, and my head rotated in the same jaunty motions as my hands. The clocks on the wall clucked and chirped and sang and bonged and chimed and ticked. The automata laughed and bowed instruments and splashed cymbals and blew trumpets. The only difference was a light on in my head. The verge of sentience.

I know it sounds strange but I am still down here. I haven't left in years. Sometimes at night I see a woman in the corner. An automata like me. She calls out to me and her voice is the muted static of the radio. Warm like crackling embers. I smell incense. I hear her laughter. But I only see her out of the corner of my eye. I must keep looking forward. I must keep moving. It is what I'm built for.

—Adam J. Galanski-De León (he/him)

—Adam J. Galanski-De León—

Swimming Pool Surgery

I lie there—bleeding heart: soaked and softened.
Somewhat removed /
lacking that awareness of mixing liquids
and plates spinning out to sea—looking
out for predators but sucked instead
to the filter and bundled just like before.
Behind strands of hair and a few loose leaves.

Hovering over the tiles and lacquer,
a few fingernails caress the divide
between rainwater / laid patterns / the rest of the body
spiraling out from the centre
of conjoined little ligaments, a connection between
the land—landscape in motion.
A little lapse in memory as the scene moves on
(elsewhere)

Inciting the chase, a little more excitement
following two figures in chase.
Heart race : foot race
Latter pulls to the front for a palpation hit.
My fingertips graze the tiles with a damp gasp
and blood races, the finale running ahead.
While mine turns to take in the damage,
unmade, making the sky glow white—
render the fat and sinew.

—Ellen Harrold—

The ~~sea-salt~~ chlorine carve of open flesh,
the eyes split open.
Wet, crimson, cracking in the oxygen path
woven in the living state.
The billows of split lungs.
Careful wear of strain,
hacking the atom thicket
with the waves of a voice soaked in lye.

—**Ellen Harrold** (she/her)

—Ellen Harrold—

The Father

> *"But if I by the finger of God cast out demons, then the Kingdom*
> *of God has come to you."* —Luke 11:20

A Catholic as a boy, says he
will worship nothing as a man, hand
inside his faithless demented devotee
until she empties upon his command
all of her demons to the rhythms of
the scripture, father and the son, always
the holy cock; he rocks, always above,
his lapsed Protestant in pigtails who plays
a parochial schoolgirl on a stage,
unconvincing atheist in the sack
beneath his immense imminence and rage,
Leviticus when at last the eyes roll back—
she spreads her legs for the apostles, grieves
these things she must suffer to once again believe.

—**Kristin Garth** (she/her)

—Kristin Garth—

Ingrid M. Calderón-Collins (she/her)

—Ingrid M. Calderón-Collins—

Bodies Bodies Bodies 19:28

> "I am here and nothing can push me aside, nothing can
> change what goes on in this world—this world is for me too,
> honey." —Octavia St. Laurent

Too many rules exist. Boundaries tailored to
regulate shapes and identities. Their whole set-

up contingent on antiquated ideologies about
how one should look or act. Must I ascribe to

these standards to be seen or am I posed struck
into the manifolds of their display cases like a

mannequin. Navigating through this gendered
and sexed landscape is like a game of Tag, I'm

it, but nobody tells me how to play. Left right
down up x y x x—where can I find the damn

cheat codes to get out of this built-in simulation—
like a strategy game, my only focus is to survive.

—**Joel Sedano** (they/them)

—Joel Sedano—

The Legend of The Webcam Killer

It was finally here, the day of the crew's annual cabin retreat. Every October David, Lacy, Mark, and Kara picked a weekend to go to the Yosemite Cabins. The stress they endured from the tests and term papers would make even the biggest philomath want to get away from it all. Drunk hookups and hangovers aside, the biggest attraction of these getaways was the terrifying fireside stories they told after sunset.

David had started this tradition. On his way to Yosemite, he thought about how this trip with his friends would probably be his last. This was their senior year in college. Ever since the pandemic, meeting up became increasingly hard, so much so that last year's trip was canceled. A year had passed since everyone last saw one another. He knew tonight would be bittersweet, but he had the perfect story for the occasion. David would go out with a bang.

Everyone arrived at the cabin around 6pm. David was the last to appear.

Mark announced excitedly, "Hey! There he is!!!"

"David! Loving the beard!" Lacy nudged him after giving him a once over with a coy look on her face.

"H-Hey guys," David stuttered.

"H-Hey Guys," Mark teased. "MAN, cheer up, CHARLIE BROWN!!! We are here to TURN UP!!! Plus, Kara has been asking about you, bro!" he said, shooting him a playful smirk.

—Chad Singleton—

Kara glared at Mark with annoyance, "Shut up, Mark!!! You're such an idiot. I did miss you Davie. Feels like it's been forever since we've talked. You look good."

"ENOUGH with the sappy bullshit. The sun is down, the fire is stoked. Grab some beers and meet me outside! IT'S SCARY STORY TIME!" asserted Mark before stepping away towards the fire pit.

The crew gathered around the blazing coals, seated comfortable in their individual chairs.

"So, who's going first?" Kara asked, scanning over the others.

David sheepishly raised his hand

"Well, whatcha got for us, Davie boy? Maybe a good vampire or ghost story?" she asked with an impatient smile.

"Um…how about a love story?"

"Oh hell no!" Mark exclaimed. "We're telling *HORROR STORIES. HORROR!* Did you not get the memo?"

David countered, "I can guarantee that this is the scariest love story you'll ever hear. It's based on a real crime of passion. AND, the killer was never found.

"NOW YOU'RE SPEAKING MY LANGUAGE DUDE!" Mark slapped his legs as he leaned in with his full attention on David.

—Chad Singleton—

The fire flickered in David's eyes. "For the sake of this story, we will call our cast of characters Kyle, Jonathan, and Cassie. Let's Begin."

***

Kyle and Jonathan were college buddies who became closer during quarantine. All of their classes were held virtually via webcam. They took Chemistry together and were assigned to be each other's partners for the semester. What started as a relationship of circumstance quickly blossomed into a strong bond. This inseparable pair would spend hours cracking jokes and gaming. Every now and then, Jonathan would see Kyle's girlfriend on camera, her name was Cassie. She had long, brown curls and piercing, green eyes. Her scarlet lips were pouty and full, forehead slightly protruding, with a little button nose. She was beautiful, and Jonathan couldn't help but notice.

At first it was an innocent crush , but Jonathan's infatuation grew. Cassie's physical beauty was only complimented by her quick wit. She reminded him a lot of Kyle. In a way, she was like one of the guys. Her and Kyle were inseparable. Jonathan would joke that if they were any closer they would be the same person.

Feelings of infatuation quickly turned into bitterness and jealousy towards Kyle.

Jonathan would often dream of a world where Cassie was his. He would fantasize about feeling her plump lips pressed against his so vividly he could almost taste her. He imagined himself on top of her warm body. Both naked forms thrusting and crashing into one another in animalistic, heated throes of passion.

After months of longing, the fantasy wasn't enough. Jonathan had to have her. In his mind, he and Cassie were meant to be.

—Chad Singleton—

Kyle and Cassie were sitting on the couch watching television when suddenly there was a knock at the door. Kyle looked through the peephole and was surprised to see Jonathan. He couldn't help but notice his friend's nervous disposition. Never had Kyle experienced such a burst of cognitive dissonance. Against all instinct, he opened the door.

Kyle's voice shook with hesitation and uncertainty.

"H-Hey...what's up, bro...What uh...brings you by?"

Jonathan shoved his way through the door, "You. Don't. Deserve her!"

Taken by surprise, Kyle stepped back. "W-What are you t-talking about Jonathan?"

"You DON'T deserve Cassie!"

Without hesitation Jonathon pulled a knife from his waist an seeing red, lunged towards Kyle—he was done talking.

Kyle had desperation in his voice and a feeling of impending doom. "WAIT!!! YOU DON'T UNDERST—"

Before Kyle could finish his sentence, Jonathan plunged the knife deep into his stomach. Blood profusely poured from Kyle's wound, he looked down grasping at his belly. He collapsed on the floor in a pool of his own blood. Cassie sat lifeless on the couch. Jonathan ran towards her, tripping over Kyle and knocking her over in the process. Jonathan watched in horror as Cassie's head fell off of her shoulders smashing into a thousand pieces upon impact with the ground. His mind didn't know what to make of this horrific scene. Her slumped over torso revealed that her back was completely hollow except for a wooden rod attached to a mechanism of levers and piano wire.

—Chad Singleton—

He gasped, "W-what...the hell is going on?"

A green eye rolled across the floor hitting Jonathan's foot with a thud, not dissimilar from a child's marble. He picked it up and noticed it was made of glass. The sudden realization of the situation made his heart sink. He thought about how inseparable Kyle and Cassie were, how she reminded him so much of Kyle. She was Kyle.

Cassie was a ventriloquist puppet created by Kyle himself.

***

David paused for a moment, "And that's—that's the whole story."

Mark clapped his hands, a tone of excitement came through his voice, "Wow! That was insane!" He cocked his head with an inquisitive expression. "Come to think of it David, I do remember hearing something about a boy from your school that was murdered about six months ago. Yeah, your school covered that story up real quick!"

Lacy inserted, "If there was a cover up—just one thing is bothering me though. How do you know so much about the story David? You talked about it as if you were there."

David stood up with tears streaming down his face. He reached in the pocket of his bubble coat, pulled out a gun, pointed it at himself with a look of determination.

"NO DAVID DON'T!!!"

—**Chad Singleton** (he/him)

—Chad Singleton—

A Beautiful Face

The keys of the piano
melodically flow, trying to steadily shatter the soprano.

Which is louder—
that which you hear,
or that which you don't?

Even when night stalks into the garden
and the moon is but a hollow hidden shape
behind a cloud—
the keys still clutter, however faint.

No amount of pitter-patter
and heavy thudding steps
ever makes it stop.

Mother calls me a liar,
and Father is too far gone
to join the debate.

The priest's hands rattle,
his tea slishes and sloshes—
the prominent slashes and slaughter
of my Father makes the holy man ponder his daughter.

—Megan Diedericks—

The piano drums on,
screeching and slicing
through the silence.

I sing Death's song—
roses and rotting corpses
are all that remain
moving on the floorboards
of this dusty tomb.

Mother comes into my room,
Father can no longer play the piano,
but why do I still hear it?

Mother touches my cheek,
stroking my statuesque skin:
"You have a face
like only a porcelain doll could—" she says.
"Haunting," she finishes.

—**Megan Diedericks** (she/her)

—Megan Diedericks—

Rabid 7:42

For the following, please provide specific grievances you would like to address:

I don't fit in. Constructs clock me like a botched nose job. Perception by any other name could be as perfect but at what cost? Being seen comes with a price like pre-packaged deals— a hodgepodge of gender and sex regulations. Yes, I could abide by these impositions onto my bodymind like a Pink Tax. But my individuality would have all too short a lease. and they couldn't get that from/for me wholesale.

—**Joel Sedano** (they/them)

—Joel Sedano—

Midsommar 47:54

Circular text (top): Gender as a cultural rite

Circular text (left): Anxieties arise like a bad trip.

Circular text (right): Rhetoric warps itself into a vortex.

Language
surrounding
gender and
sex get knotted
together like ribbons around the maypole. Am I enough? Do I fit in?
Must abide to
instructions
like a dance.
Follow crumbs
to their
prescription.
Rules set in
place
passing
as tradition.
Dizzying
round and
round
and round,
what does
it take
to be
crowned
May Queen?
Like garlands
I am mal-
lleable but
how much
should I
ascribe to
cult
behavior?
If I am forced to
participate
in their
games, am
I really auto-
nomous in
making my
own choices?

—Joel Sedano (they/them)

—Joel Sedano—

Deer in the Headlights
—Petra-Jurik Dracovich (he/they/it)

—Petra-Jurik Dracovich—

Glass

It didn't make much of a noise, this crime of gravity. I stood, stock still, the liquid pooling, a charge of instantaneous damage against the wooden floor.

Already the voices were raised.

I took the rag from my apron and dropped it around the edge of the oozing. My foot guided the towel around the growing border, trying to sop it back toward its center where it could be contained. By now the voices had multiplied. Loud, gruff, brisk, they demanded I do better. They accused me of being lazy, inexperienced, unqualified. They shouted that the liquid was secondary; the glass was the main culprit.

Again I surrounded the liquid, making a smaller and smaller diameter until it was a manageable circle. Saturated, I attempted to stand in order to ring out the towel in a nearby sink but the voices, which had dulled to a soft murmur, rose in protest to this action. Few words could be understood among the roar but I knew if I completed my intended action I would be reprimanded. My towel fell with a flat slosh and I returned to the floor before a pile of jagged edges.

I grabbed at the pieces with soft fingers, slipping one sliver at a time into my apron pocket, taking care not to tear the fabric. The chatter that surrounded me began to grow, not in volume from individuals but from a growing population. I stared at the floor as their broken reflections discussed the method with which I cleared the mess.

Then all progress was lost. One of them, or perhaps a small group, barked, deep and guttural, in clear opposition to

—Padraig Hogan—

my actions. Coupled with the call was a bright shattering. Or several in quick succession. Since I refused to do it right the first time, they justified, I would keep working at it until I learned.

Glass surrounded me, flying across my hands and face. I shut my eyes, but too late, as behind the tightness of my eyelids I felt a sharp pressure. They opened to a view of bifurcated red. I used two fingers to hold it open and began digging around for the culprit with the other. The slice felt both nowhere and everywhere. I hovered a finger just above my eye, searching for any protrusion. A shiver ran through me when I found it. My fingernails were just long enough to pinch the end. I grasped at the air, seeking the line between missing entirely and further damage.

Behind me the pack grew louder, howling and yelping. It continued to grow in size too; even without sight I knew that.

My eye, dry from the minutes without blinking, watered to compensate. The tears that didn't drip onto the glass ran into my mouth, leaving with them the diluted taste of metal.

When my fingers found the sharpness, all went silent. I pulled in no rush, wanting to ensure my safety. The jagged edges of the glass made it impossible to know from which direction it had entered. I tried to pull it straight out but the slightest bit of resistance made me wary. Moving it from side to side did little to alleviate this.

I accepted that I would have to pull hard, away from me, just once.

—Padraig Hogan—

Everything was numb, then red, then dark as I squeezed my eyes shut. It took a moment for the pain to find me, but it always finds me. I flinched against what was inside of me.

Everyone was quiet until I tried to stand. I slipped back down and tried to feel for the shards to collect, but my loss of vision made this impossible. Trying to traverse the pointed landscape, my foot found the towel and slipped, landing me in a jagged pile.

Glass penetrated my hands at every angle. A group behind me gave a small bit of applause.

I slammed my palms into the floor and the clapping spread.

I used my arms to gather what glass I could and rolled them over the pile, then my chest and back, legs and feet. The noise was deafening until it wasn't. When I had every last bit of glass in me.

—**Padraig Hogan** (he/him)

—Padraig Hogan—

Dad Speaks

shut up | shut up | shut *up* | i love you honey | you think this is yelling i can
show you what yelling sounds like | don't look at me like that | don't
look away | look at me when i'm talking to you | look me in the eye

shut up | hush up | bite your tongue | you better watch your mouth | you
think that's funny huh | wait till we get home you wont be laughing then |
what is your problem | have you lost your mind | stop being
melodramatic | snap out of it | sit on your hands | ill deal with you later |
did you hear what i said | don't say yes say yes sir | yes sir | yes
sir | look me in the eye | you did great today | you look nice | oh you think
you're smart | think you know better than your father |
you can do better | try harder | go back to bed

need a little motivation huh | need something to help you remember |
stop screaming or you're gonna get more | knock it off | get control of yourself |
quit acting like a baby | i love you too honey | drive safe | lock your doors |
you are exceptionally intelligent | you think you know better than your father
do you | you got a problem huh you got a problem | you disobey you get
the consequences | keep moving around like that and it'll hurt worse | be careful
driving home | quit overreacting | i *warned* you | maybe next time
you'll think twice | i'm really proud of you honey | get back in here | where do you
think you're going | shut up | look me in the eye

—**Sophie Farthing** (she/her)

—Sophie Farthing—

Doesn't the Moon Look Beautiful Tonight?

"Would you like to join me?"

Moonlight sweeps the aisle of the bus, revealing, across from him, a young woman clad in a stellar leather jacket.

"If you don't mind."

"Wouldn't have asked if I did," she assures him with a smile, coaxing him over with a slight beckon of the hand.

He climbs over the empty seat beside him and crosses the aisle to claim the one next to her. The bus driver takes a quick look through the oblong mirror above him, more out of boredom than concern for the movements of his passengers.

"What were you reading?" Her eyes are dark, pupils lost within iris like curious black holes. He likes the way nothing reflects through them, like they eat up everything.

"I can't quite remember," he replies with a nervous tremor.

She notices. "I don't bite. I'm just not tired, and we have a long way to go. You looked like you were in the same boat."

He takes a deep breath and lets it out with a sigh, allowing himself to relax. "I can't sleep in vehicles. Never could. I always think of that Final Destination movie where the—"

"Logs fall off the truck and decimate the car full of people? Yeah, I remember that one," she giggles.

"Right. I guess in my mind, if I'm awake, I can at least react if something like that happens."

—Cole Martin—

"What are you going to do, Van Damme? Jump out the window? We're going like a hundred clicks an hour—probably twenty over knowing Lenny."

"Lenny?"

"The driver. He always runs this route."

He likes how curly her hair is. It's like hundreds of Slinkies let loose to gravity. He follows them with his eyes like they're spiraling roller coasters.

She upsets the spectacle. "What are you looking at?"

"I was following the curls of your hair like they were spiraling roller coasters," he responds earnestly.

"How literary." She laughs with big bright teeth, teasing him.

The bumpy road does little to rouse the other passengers from their sleep. It's a dreamy world full of dreamy people. A shooting star arcs the sky for a little too long.

"Doesn't the moon look beautiful tonight?" she asks, disrupting his wandering mind.

"I love you too," he says before he can stop himself.

She giggles at him, and his face flushes red and hot. He begins to backpedal.

"Sorry, I...I didn't mean to...It's a famous Japanese translation," he vomits.

"A famous Japanese translation of what?" She speaks through giggles like they're their own language, decipherable only in short bursts. His cheeks feel like they're sun burnt.

—Cole Martin—

"'I love you'. I think the story goes that there isn't really a direct translation of 'love', so 'isn't the moon beautiful tonight?' was someone's crack at it. Can't remember their name, though."

She chuckles once more and brushes a few curls from her eyes. "I think everyone understands love—it only gets complicated when words come into the picture."

He smiles, his embarrassment lessening a little now that he's plead his case. "Well put," he states.

Lenny guides the bus along the phantom road, parting the ocean of trees at either side. There's something peculiar about the silence of the cabin; the drone of the tires melts into a dissonant drawl. He decides not to think about it too much.

"You haven't asked me where I'm going," she chimes at him.

"I figured we're going to the same place," he retorts.

"What makes you say that?"

"A feeling."

"It's good to trust those."

"Sometimes."

They share a smile.

He sinks into his seat. His body makes an impression in the leather, a comfortable little nest. Maybe he'll stay here awhile. He feels like there's no meaning to a destination, the same way the destination of a shooting star means nothing—it's brilliant just in its moment, and to think of its end means to

—*Cole Martin*—

kill it right then and there. He thinks of swimming in rivers and sitting in bed with tomato soup. He thinks of tall trees and Chamomile tea. He thinks of roller coasters and pretty girls with pretty, curly hair. He thinks of cute old people and barking puppies and holding hands at the movies—all things like shooting stars. He thinks he might be dead, but mostly he thinks he thinks too much. He doesn't think of where he's going.

He turns to her. "Who are you?"

"Does it matter?"

"Kind of." He wipes his eyes. He feels tired. The air is heavy.

"Just relax. You're playing your part," she replies, stroking his hair.

His words are a slurred mess. "Why do I feel so tired?"

The aisle of the bus shifts, extending and retracting simultaneously, like a dolly shot. He notices people he hadn't noticed before. A handful of elderlies litter the seats in front, their heads turned toward him with piercing, empty eyes. He looks to the rearview mirror and Lenny looks back at him, his eyes gone, replaced by hollow sockets—his skin melted down to the bone.

"What's h-happening..." Each word feels like an insurmountable effort.

"Shhhh...It'll be over soon." She runs her hands along his cheek, and her once darkened eyes are alight with flaming coronas.

—*Cole Martin*—

He drags his eyes ahead once more. The elderly inhabitants grin at him, their wrinkled and saggy skin receding until taut and unblemished. His heartbeat is faint—the periodic slam of a distant bass drum. His hands shrivel and his fragile bones crack and break, his body collapsing in on itself.

His last remaining strength escapes his lips in a query, "Why?"

"Because honey, to get to where they want to go," she nods to the now youthful passengers of the bus, "they need to be beautiful. *Perfect*. But beauty," She leans in closely and whispers wetly into his ear, "requires vitality. We need people like *you*." She boops his nose with her finger, crumbling it to dust. "Our little Goldilocks. You're fuel to get us where we're going; cattle for the righteous soul." She shines him that winning smile.

The world becomes distant. He feels shrunken, sucked into the seat like a great vacuum has opened beneath him. Through the window, another shooting star is snuffed out by the sky.

—**Cole Martin** (he/him)

—Cole Martin—

The Red Queen
—**Carella Keil** (she/her)

—Carella Keil—

Heat Death

Darkness
sears flesh.
Come to bed
but first, turn
out the lights.
Let me smell
you in the sizzle
of smoke-coated
phantoms
while we scream
in unison.
Let us die
before we see
what feeds
on the hot
supper-steam
of us.

—Jennifer Ruth Jackson (she/her)

—Jennifer Ruth Jackson—

The Curse of Joseph Henry Loveless

You drive us along highways throughout the West Coast, searching for the dismembered remains of an outlaw who craved the silent moon, its fullness persuading him to butcher his wife with an ax. Decades earlier, a young girl searching for arrowheads in a cave discovered his torso in a burlap sack, his skull never found, a souvenir your father hungered for.

I choke on rotted honeydew, a flower crown knotted in my filthy hair. The forceful way you entered my life reminds me of a movie: a dying man kissing a woman, the hauntings of the hotel replacing her blooming skin with decaying flesh.

The constellations in the night sky begin to dim, allowing shooting stars to release fairy dust. A song from 1968 whispers from the radio and rouses memories of childish hands burying a mother's secret in the backyard, the morning fog thickening with the saliva of famished men.

As we drive through California, I imagine the landscape burning, destroying any evidence of a careless man's skull.

—Chimen Georgette Kouri (she/her)

—Chimen Georgette Kouri—

ABOUT THE CONTRIBUTORS

❖ After falling in love with The Spiderwick Chronicles, A.J. Cossey (she/they) always had a bit of a thing for the supernatural and spooky. She has boundless love for the LGBTQ+ community. Marrying queerness and horror as her main body of work just seemed right. It was difficult for Alannah to find queer fiction in the West Midlands, UK growing up. She wants to create characters that would have made her feel seen and listened to. Eventually, she hopes to make the West Midlands a bit less grey and a lot more gay.

❖ Adam J. Galanski-De León (he/him) is the author of "The Magpie Funeral" (Querencia Press), and the forthcoming novel, "Szarotka" (American Buffalo Books). His work has appeared in Farside Review, Masks, the Running Wild Press Novella Anthology, and other journals. He lives in Chicago, IL with his wife and four cats. Adam maintains a website at http://www.adamjgalanskideleon.com.

❖ Areeba Zanub (she/her) is a Pakistani-American writer and artist who was raised in New York City. She studied English at CUNY Brooklyn College and is interested in topics relating to mental health, generational trauma, girlhood, and philosophy. Instagram: @motheatencurtain

❖ Ariya Bandy is a writer of fiction and poetry who loves to surround herself with many types of literature. Her work appears in Iceblink Literary Magazine, Moonbow Magazine, and elsewhere.

❖ Blayne Waterloo (they/she) is a horror writer and editor living in Georgia with their partner and loud dog.

❖ Carella is a writer and digital artist who creates surreal, dreamy images that explore nature, fantasy realms, portraiture, melancholia and inner dimensions. She has been published in numerous literary journals including Columbia Journal, Chestnut Review and Crannóg. Her writing was recently nominated for a Pushcart Prize, and she is a 2023 Door is a Jar Award Winner. Her art has appeared on the covers of Glassworks Magazine, Nightingale and Sparrow, Colors: The Magazine, Frost Meadow Review and Straylight Magazine. instagram.com/catalogue.of.dreams – twitter.com/catalogofdream

- ❖ Carson Sandell (they/them) is a queer and trans poet from San Jose, CA. They graduated from University of California Riverside with a B.A. in Creative Writing. Carson is a first year MFA Candidate in Poetry at San Diego State University. Outside of academics they are a Poetry Reader for Split Lip Magazine and Poetry Editor at Poetry is Currency. Most nights you will find them curled up watching a horror movie.

- ❖ Chad Singleton is a Public Health Scientist, published Children's Book Author and a Horror Writer. His interests include voice over , music and podcasting. He is currently working towards his Doctorate in Public Health at Walden University.

- ❖ Chimen Georgette Kouri is a Pushcart-nominated writer based in Cliffwood Beach, New Jersey. She is the author of the chapbook *Peach Milk* (Bottlecap Press, 2021) and the poetry and prose collection *What Haunts Me the Most* (Querencia Press, 2023). She fell in love with storytelling one Christmas morning during a power outage when she and her parents laid in bed while her father told stories about his life in Lebanon. She is writing another full-length poetry and prose collection, *The Old Dutchburn House*, and co-writing a romance series with her boyfriend, which they hope to finish soon. When she isn't writing, you can find her cuddling her dogs and cats and rewatching *The Last Kingdom* on Netflix.

- ❖ Cole Martin is a twenty-something writer from Atlantic Canada. He has words in The Ekphrastic Review, healthline zine, Fahmidan Journal, Rejection Letters, Bulb Culture Collective, and more. He can be found on Twitter @maritimemagnate, and on Substack (asilaytrying.substack.com)

- ❖ Cromika works with whatever materials she has on hand. She began crocheting when she was nine years old. Now, with twenty years of experience and her volunteer role at Mecca in Eugene, she now has access to more fun and frivolous embellishments. She likes the fun of the go-with-the-flow nature of having access to scrap yarns both from Mecca and Goodwill: "it's a surprise grab-bag, you never know what you're going to end up with". The freedom of expression that comes from the chaotic choices available is part of the magic that makes these crochet creatures, garments and work of art distinctly Cromika. https://cromika.weebly.com/

- ❖ Cypress Wilde (they/them) is a disabled and queer author and artist based in New Jersey. They have their first chapbook, *I'm Stuck in Limbo, But Please Don't Save Me.* published with Bottlecap Press. As for art, they have published with Bullshit Lit, Moss Puppy Mag, Same Faces Collective, Koru Magazine, and Zene Magazine. Cypress is constantly creating, with a focus on the environment and lived experiences as a disabled person. During their free time they sell zines and stickers at local markets in New Jersey and Philly. You can find them on instagram @behemothlullabies & @queercriprecords.

❖ Eliza is a current graduate student at UIC program for writers. A Queer and neurodivergent writer, much of her work looks at the mysteries hidden within the mundane, peeling back the trivialities of daily life to reveal something new and strange. She examines ritual and routine as forces to be personified with lives and dreams of their own. Eliza is the author of *You Shouldn't Worry About the Frogs* her debut short story collection published by Querencia Press. Her work has also appeared in independent journals such as Red Ogre Review and Chaotic Merge Magazine. In her spare time Eliza plays the harp and is an avid reader of folklore and mysteries. Eliza enjoys hiking, kayaking, and baking. She can often be found with a cup of tea and her cat, Theo, laying on top of her laptop while she tries to edit.

❖ Ellen Harrold (She/her) is an artist, writer, and editor of Metachrosis Literary. She is currently exploring the connections between science, art, and storytelling. She has recently published poetry with *Die Leere Mitte, New Note Poetry,* and *Skylight 47.* She also published her first book 'The Aesthetics and Conventions of Medical Art.

❖ Hana Carolina (she/her) is a pseudonym of an Edinburgh-based creative and academic writer. Born in Poland, she moved to Scotland and studied literature, film, and television for many years. Since then, she's been working as a tutor, interpreter, researcher, and publishing academically while dreaming of writing dark stories about horrible people.

❖ Ingrid M. Calderón-Collins is a poet, tarot reader, editor-in-chief of resurrection magazine & the hostess of SERPENTINE reading series at north figueroa bookshop. She is the author of twenty-six poetry books and lives in Los Angeles, CA.

❖ Irina Tall (Novikova) is an artist, graphic artist, illustrator. She graduated from the State Academy of Slavic Cultures with a degree in art, and also has a bachelor's degree in design. The first personal exhibition "My soul is like a wild hawk" (2002) was held in the museum of Maxim Bagdanovich. In her works, she raises themes of ecology, in 2005 she devoted a series of works to the Chernobyl disaster, draws on anti-war topics. The first big series she drew was The Red Book, dedicated to rare and endangered species of animals and birds. Writes fairy tales and poems, illustrates short stories. She draws various fantastic creatures: unicorns, animals with human faces, she especially likes the

—Contributors—

image of a man - a bird - Siren. In 2020, she took part in Poznań Art Week. Her work has been published in magazines: Gypsophila, Harpy Hybrid Review, Little Literary Living Room and others. In 2022, her short story was included in the collection "The 50 Best Short Stories", and her poem was published in the collection of poetry "The wonders of winter".

❖ Jack is a queer poet interested in writing about folklore and repurposing the Irish folk tradition. They have work published in the bolton review, natalogue and the P.N. Review.

❖ Jennifer Ruth Jackson writes about reality's weirdness and the plausibility of the fantastic. Her work has appeared in *Strange Horizons*, *Star*Line*, *Apex Magazine*, and more. When she isn't writing, you can find her crafting a variety of things or playing video games with her husband. Visit her on Twitter: @jenruthjackson.

❖ Jessica Drake-Thomas is a poet, novelist, and PhD student. She is the author of two poetry collections, *Burials* and *Bad Omens*, as well as one novel, *Hollow Girls*. She is the poetry editor at *Coffin Bell Journal*. Her work has been nominated for the Best of the Net, the Rhysling Award, and the Elgin Award. She lives in Milwaukee with Nick and their two dogs, Poppy and Potato.

❖ Joel Sedano (they/them) is a queer, trans non-binary, disabled Chicanx reconnecting to their Indigenous roots in Western Guanajuato. They are a poet, photographer, performer, director, painter, and beader. Joel's poetry has been featured in Phineas Literary Magazine, Art of Writing Anthology, and Love and Pride: The Musical's "We're a Rainbow Section," Semana de la Mujer Journal, Olney Magazine, Honey Literary Magazine, Cordite Poetry Review, and No, Dear Magazine. Joel debuted their short film "Post-Prismatic" at the 2020 Queer Women of Color Film Festival. They are also a landscape photographer with works published in Lux the Zine and WerkHaus Zine.

❖ Josh Dale (he/him) is a native Pennsylvanian and the author of the novella, The Light to Never Be Snuffed (Alien Buddha Press, 2022), and the poetry collection, Duality Lies Beneath (Thirty West Publishing, 2016). He hopes you read them outside, far away from society, and maybe with a cat. Say hi at www.joshdale.co

❖ Kristin Garth is a womanchildish Pushcart, Rhysling nominated sonneteer and a Best of the Net 2020 finalist, the author of DADDY (Anxiety Press) and 27 other books of poetry and prose.

—Contributors—

❖ Leah Barron is a poet from Yorkshire, England. She is a horror fan and part of the goth subculture. As a creative writing graduate, she has used poetry in mental health recovery.

❖ Native New Yorker LindaAnn LoSchiavo (she/her), a four time nominee for The Pushcart Prize, was also nominated for Best of the Net, Balcones Poetry Prize, an Ippy, a Firecracker Award, the Rhysling Award, and Dwarf Stars. She is a member of SFPA, British Fantasy Society, and The Dramatists Guild. Titles for 2022: "Women Who Were Warned" (Cerasus Poetry) and "Messengers of the Macabre: Hallowe'en Poems" (Audience Askew). Forthcoming in 2023: "Apprenticed to the Night" (UniVerse Press), "Felones de Se: Poems about Suicide" (Ukiyoto Publishing), and "Vampire Ventures" (Alien Buddha Press). Forthcoming in 2024: "Cancer Courts My Mother" (Penumbra / Stanislaus State College).

❖ Megan Diedericks writes poetry and fiction, everything from meek to macabre can be found in between the lines. She has a poetry collection available on Amazon, and her work has been published by *fifth wheel press*, *Last Leaves Magazine* and her short horror story won *Tales from the Moonlit Path's 2022 Halloween challenge.* Visit her website (bit.ly/megandiedericks) for more information, or find her on Instagram (@meganreflects)!

❖ Nayt Rundquist (they/them) is a writer, editor, anthologist, and professor. Their odd scribblings can be found in *Inverted Syntax*, *Digging Through the Fat*, *Roi Fainéant*, *Scavengers Lit Mag*, *Fast Flesh Literary*, *The Citron* Review, and anthologized at Querencia Press and in *Unbound: Composing Home* (New Rivers Press 2022). They live just outside space and time with their artist-jeweler wife and their fifth-dimensional dogs.

❖ Padraig Hogan is an author and musician from the foothills outside Yosemite, CA. He has a BA in English and Philosophy from Fresno State University and an MFA in Creative Writing from The California Institute of the Arts. His debut short story collection *Wax* was released through Querencia Press in 2022. When he isn't writing stories or music, he is spoiling his cat Logan. He currently teaches English at Nevada State University.

❖ Paula Charles has spent much of her life reading and writing under the towering trees of the Pacific Northwest. She has a love for pie, small towns, family history, and the possibility of ghosts. When she's not reading or writing, she can usually be found in the kitchen, baking up a sweet treat. Paula lives on a small farm in southwestern Washington with her husband and a plethora of fuzzy and feathered critters. She is the author of the Hometown Hardware cozy mystery series, as well as the forthcoming Zen Goat cozy mystery series written under the pen name of Janna Rollins. Her work has been published in Yellow Mama Press.

❖ Petra-Jurik Dracovich (he/they/it), known online as ScleraCentipede, is a multimedia artist and slow-fashion maker originally from Azerbaijan living in the UK. Their art explores lust and horror. the intersection between desire and disgust through a queer, kink lens. He is currently developing its practice alongside its studies of BA Creative Arts with the Open College of The Arts, community organising, and work in the voluntary sector.

❖ Samuel Cooley (he/him) is a writer, editor, and actor raised in Vidalia, Louisiana. He is an alumnus of Louisiana Tech University and is currently pursuing his MFA at the University of New Orleans. His work can be found in *Daikaijuzine, Ellipsis,* and *The Quatrain.*

❖ Sarah Kuntz is a horror author living in Orlando, Florida. Exploring the nuances of disability is important to them and they create content solely focused on the intersection between disability and horror on their blog sarahhaunts.me.

❖ Sarah R. New (she/her) has been writing since the age of 6. Sarah loves to cook and is an avid traveler who has visited four continents. Her travel memoir, *The Great European Escape: The Trials and Tribulations of Travelling While Chronically Ill,* is available for free from https://sarahrnew.wordpress.com/.

❖ Sophie Farthing (she/her) is a queer writer living in South Carolina. Her work is forthcoming or has appeared in outlets including Impostor Journal, Beyond Queer Words, and Anti-Heroin Chic.

❖ Stephanie Parent is an author of fiction and poetry. Her newest release, the creative nonfiction chapbook *My Dungeon Love Affair,* is forthcoming in June 2024 from Stanchion Books.

❖ Stephanie Ritzema is a 23-year-old poet and creative writer living in London and studying on the ICE Cambridge Creative Writing Masters. She is deeply interested in writing that confronts perceptions of the female-presenting body and its links to both science fiction and folklore. She has written dark fantasy, horror and science fiction for years and has been experimenting with transgressing genre throughout her poetry and prose.

❖ Tinamarie Cox (she/her) lives in Arizona with her (very much alive) husband and two (not as finicky anymore) children. Her written and visual work has appeared in numerous publications under a variety of genres. She is also the author of a poetry chapbook, *Self-Destruction in Small Doses*. Find more of her work at tinamariethinkstoomuch.weebly.com.

❖ Victoria Hood (she/her) is the author of a collection of short stories *My Haunted Home* (FC2) and chapbooks *Death and Darlings* and *Entries of Boredom and Fear* (Bottlecap Press). Her book of poetry, *I Am My Mothers Disappointments*, is forthcoming from Girl Noise Press (2024). She hopes to discomfort, humor, and charm.

❖ Vix Martin is a new author ready to captivate and disgust readers with body horror narratives that grab the reader to yank them down to unexplored depths. Exploring their queer identity and how it relates to their OCD and BPD causes their stories to reflect a kaleidoscope of emotions, merging the terror within the mind with the grotesque transformations of the body. Martin's work not only pushes the boundaries of horror literature but also serves as a cathartic exploration of mental illness and trauma.

—Contributors—